The Pocket Fairies of Middleburg

The Pocket Fairies of Middlebury

A Tale of the Little Folk in the Here-Now Time

Linda L. Zern

illustrated by Linda S. Day

LinWood House Publishing 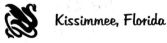 Kissimmee, Florida

The Pocket Fairies of Middleburg
©2004 Linda Zern

Editors: Cherilyn King, Paula Kalinoski
Illustrator: Linda S. Day
Interior and Cover Design: MyLinda Butterworth of
                                            Day to Day Enterprises
Design Edit: Phillip Stahle
Cover Photography: Maren Zern

ISBN # 0-9753098-0-3
LCCN # 2004092351

Printed in the United States of America
10 9 8 7 6 5 4 3 2 1

Published by LinWood House Publishing
Kissimmee, Florida

This book is for my first grandchild, Zoe Baye Stahle,
and all the grandchildren yet to be.

A word fitly spoken is like apples of gold in pictures of silver.
Proverbs 25:11

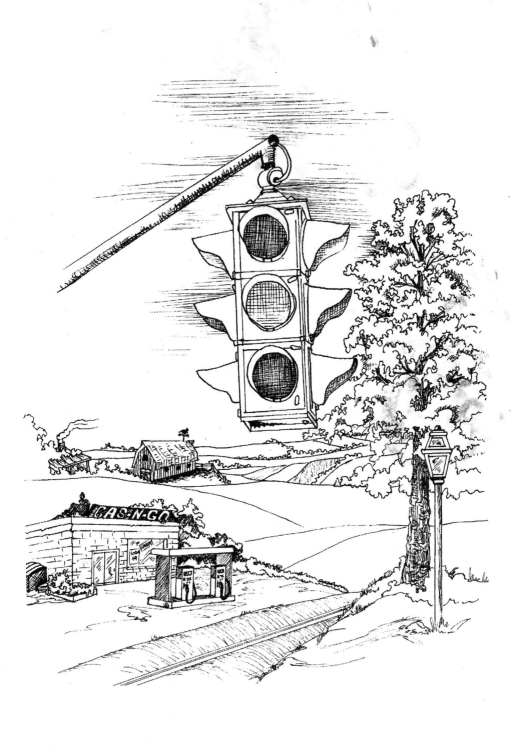

The Story Before the Story

The Prologue

I n the middle of Middleburg, in the middle of Middle Street, at the very center of the intersection, a pair of pocket fairies built their nest. In the one and only traffic light in Middleburg, Marker, the fathling, and Nanda, his wifely, built a lovely nest out of moss, strands of pony hair, and the pinfeathers of Muscovy ducks. Muscovy duck feathers are a favorite for fairy nests, of course, because Muscovy ducks cannot quack, and so they have no mischief-magic to disturb young nestling fairies.

Marker Best Moon and Nanda Star Shimmer of the Sky Weaver Night Shine clan tried to be both wise and careful when it came to things like nest building and raising their younglings.

Pocket fairies, in the back-before time, were happy to settle into the hoods or pockets of forgotten coats, cloaks, and capes. Sometimes they would nest in worn out shoes left by humans—mostly farmers and their families. Pocket fairies, unlike attic sprites and tree stump pixies, enjoyed being close to humans and called them the pocklings. In that back-before time, it hadn't been completely unheard of for some farmer's wife to come upon an abandoned fairy nest in a winter coat or cloak. Never suspecting pocket fairies, that good wife would shake out bits of twig and string from her family's clothing during spring cleaning and assume that some bird or mouse had left its nest behind.

In the oldest of times, before humans even had pockets, a fairy family would settle near the chimney of a hut or cottage in the summer or under a cow's manger in the winter to raise their nestlings. Pocket fairies were happy to bring their human family a touch of fairy luck and a little dreamly magic. This has been true everywhere and for always.

The world has changed a lot from the days of comfortable chimneys and the deep pockets of farmers' forgotten coats. Today, pocket fairies improvise and try to settle just about anywhere that is safe and dry. Nanda and Marker did not long for the old days and ways; they liked to think of themselves as newly fairy folk. They enjoyed being part of the modern world, or what they called the newly time, and its peculiar magic—like wondrous traffic lights that shine day and night and forever, or so it seemed.

Nanda and Marker had three nestlings in their first litter. The oldest nestling, by one minute and three-eighths of a second, they named Gennis Star Milk after Nanda's godmotherly. Gennis looked like her motherly and had Nanda's long chestnut hair and spark-blue eyes. In her up-grown time, she would be very slender and tall like Nanda. For now, she was thin and somewhat smallish. When Gennis grew wings they would be an iridescent blue on top and white underneath like her fathling's and not a glowing orange-brown and slashing black like her motherly's. She was serious minded like her motherly, but she often liked to think up stories just like her fathling. As the first born nestling, she was often the first to be given new responsibilities. Sometimes this pleased Gennis, and other times she wished she might be last at something.

The second nestling, a brotherling, Nanda and Marker named Paunch Moon Climb, because they liked the solid ring of it, and the way the name Paunch rhymed with solid words like staunch and launch. A happy, sky-straight nestling, Paunch liked to eat and laugh. He often found his own jokes very funny. Paunch's hair was the deep brown of a pine knot and it grew in pointy, spiked clumps. His eyes were the color of green moss water.

Paunch would look just like his fathling someday, but for now he was a little boney in the knees and a little clumsy in the feet. He often vexed his motherly, who was sure he was going to fall out of the nest because of sheer silliness. Paunch frequently made his fathling laugh.

The third and youngest nestling in the litter was named Jolly Sky Glint after Marker's sisterly and motherly. Just like her Aunt Jolly, Jolly Sky Glint was a beautiful, golden pocket fairy with flash-white hair and amber eyes. Jolly sometimes thought too much about her looks and had to be reminded, at times, to be less vain, but because she had a goodly heart she always tried to do better.

Jolly worked hard at learning the art of weaving spider silk cloth with her motherly, and had already made a traveling cloak for her fathling. Jolly liked it when her fathling praised her for her tight, even stitches. His praise-pat made her heart feel full and warm.

✤

Marker and Nanda's family loved their nest in the sky. Fathling called their nest cozy. Motherly called it just right. They both called it tight-fast. On lazy days, the sky-nest swayed easily in the warm breeze, lulling the young ones into a singing sleep. Long ago a family of finches had nested in the traffic light, and for a few seasons a pair of squirrels had raised their babies there. Now the traffic light nicely suited the family of Marker and Nanda.

All day and all night, the old traffic light glowed—red, green, yellow and then back to red. Spilling through rusty cracks into the nest, a few stray light beams flashed bright and constant over the nestlings, keeping them warm and making their motherly's wings glow.

Hanging high in the sky over Middleburg, the family of Nanda and Marker Sky Weaver Night Shine was safe from the flesh-scratchers who meowed of their hunger and scratched at their fleas behind the *Gas-N-Go*. They were safe from the swallowers that shed their skins and slithered in the shadows of the wide-big open. They were safe, and they were heart-bound to each other.

Gennis, Paunch, and Jolly, in their fairy nest above Middle Street, drank the milk of mice, ate quick-grass bread, and waited impatiently for their wings to grow.

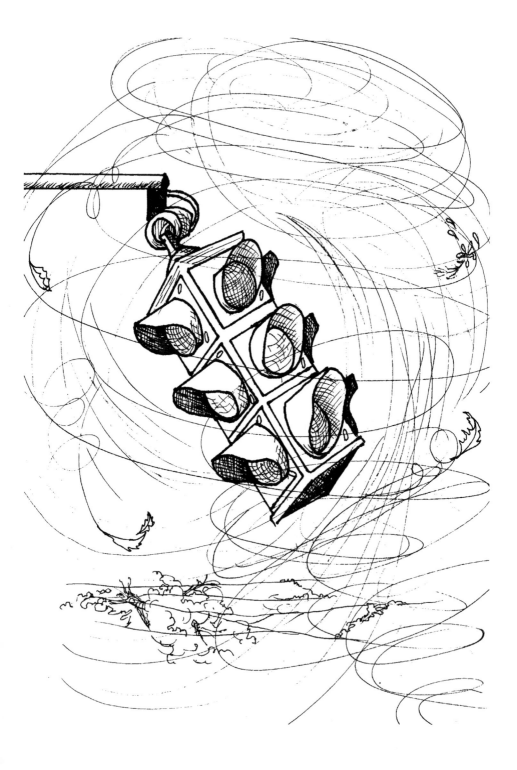

Chapter One

Zebra Dust in the Wild Salt Wind

The wind shrieked and beat at the traffic light like a fist.
"Gennis, hear me."
The nest tipped farther on its side. Gennis hugged Paunch and Jolly, squeezing them hard. The three fairy nestlings braced themselves against each other as their nest rolled and pitched and tipped and rattled. Frightened, Gennis had her eyes as squint-tight as she could squeeze them.

"Gennis Star Milk, look at me!" Nanda, their motherly, yelled over the shriek of the wind. The wind shrieked louder. "Do not leave the nest, Gennis. Keep your brotherling and sisterly tight-fast in the nest. Stay tight until your fathling and I return."

Opening her eyes, Gennis could just make out her motherly in the darkly gloom. Nanda carried her long bow in one hand and a charm sack on her shoulder. Through the entryway of their nest Gennis could see a mad swirling of gray rain and wind. Her motherly had to crawl down against the crazy tip of their home to reach the opening in the bottom. Like a kite flying on a string, the traffic light flew on its tether in the terrible storm. The wall became the floor, and the floor became the wall, and rain leaked in through cracks, holes, and hidden places. Clumps of moss and pinfeathers clung to her motherly's gown and wings.

Nanda cautioned Paunch, "You must help Gennis while I search for Fathling."

Water dripped from the end of Paunch's nose as he said, "Motherly, I will be as bravely as I can be."

Nanda smiled. Paunch could still make her smile, even as the wild-salt-wind tore at their nest, and fear tore at Nanda's heart for Marker, who had been missing now for a gone-long day and a night.

"I know that you will be as bravely as you can," she said, brushing a clump of hair from his face.

Jolly's small voice asked from the wet-dark, "Motherly, will the nest fall?"

"Your fathling has chosen a goodly nest, Jolly sweetling. Have no worry-concern about that. And we will be back soon, and then Fathling can tell you the story about how he found this beautiful sky-nest for you." Nanda knew that the promise of a story was sometimes the best of comforts for young fairy nestlings.

"I will be bravely, too," Gennis said, but she was cold, and her teeth chattered as she said it.

Lightening slashed outside, and the nestlings flinched when the thunder cracked. To Gennis Nanda repeated, "Keep tight-fast in the nest."

To Paunch and Jolly she said, "Listen to Gennis. You must give heed to your sisterly. You three must wait-fast. I have more than courage with which to find your fathling. Do not fear about that. The nest will hold, and I will find him."

Gennis nodded when her motherly touched her wet cheek and whispered that she should not be afraid. But Gennis was afraid, too afraid now to close her eyes. Gennis stared hard as her motherly stretched her wings and flew into the churning, tearing, midnight-wind. The wind shrieked and beat at the traffic light like a fist. The nestlings grabbed tight-fast to each other and waited in the dark-alone.

When the wind had just started to blow—in the beginning, gently—it had smelled of mermaids and salt and something dark and wild. Fathling explained that the smell was snips of flutterlys' wings and bits of stone-strong trunkleys' eyelashes, all mixed with the dust made by the black-white stripelys who dance in the dirt.

He had taught them what pocklings call the black-white stripelys—zebras—he had said. The nestlings had laughed at the silly word. He also told them about rise-high flyers with great, fringed wings that could never fly and animals with necks so long that they are able to nibble on the tops of trees. The nestlings' eyes had been moon-wide as he taught them about the wide-big world far beyond their nest in Middleburg.

Fathling had told them it was a very big wind that could bring dust from the land of the dirt-dancing stripelys. He had not heard of such a darkly wind in a very long time. Not since he was a nestling could he remember smelling zebra dust on the wild-salt-wind.

At first it had excited the nestlings when their nest started to sway in the saltly wind. Paunch made a game of it. He rolled forth and back until Jolly and Gennis complained and Motherly scolded. When Fathling pat-kissed the three of them goodbye and promised to bring them sweet treats from the orange tree seed, they laughed and clapped. Fathling wanted to gather extra food before the wild-salt-zebra-wind grew too strong for a pocket fairy to fly against. He hug-kissed their motherly and promised to hurry home before the wind grew too dangerous.

When their fathling had been gone for a long time, and the wind had tipped the nest so far on its side that Gennis, Paunch, and Jolly fell down sprawling, the nestlings began to have some worry-concern. Still their fathling had not come home. When Jolly got slammed against the wall and bruised her elbow, the nestlings worried a little more, and still their fathling had not come home. When the rain began to blow right into the nest and soaked their nightshirts, the nestlings were sick with worry-concern, and still their fathling had not returned.

Nanda could not remember so rant-wild a rain in her whole life. She kissed the bruised knees and scraped elbows of her nestlings and tried to imagine where Marker could be in all that gray, wild rain. Nanda's worry-concern became so great she thought she could hear Marker calling to her on the wind, but she couldn't be sure. If he was hurt he would need her healing magic, but she did not want to leave her shake-afraid nestlings. Nanda kissed bruised elbows and scraped knees and strained to hear messages on the wind, trying to decide who needed her the most and how she could help them all.

By the time Nanda decided to go in search of Marker, the wind had been blowing for such a long time that Gennis, Paunch, and Jolly lost all sense of day-night. The red, yellow, and green lights had long since gone dark.

After their motherly had gone to search for their fathling, the nestlings were so wet and so tired that at first they could not sleep. But finally they did.

Still later, in the dark-alone, while the wind shrieked in their tired ears, they dreamed of strange striped animals with too smallish wings that flew thousands of miles to kidnap and carry them away. And still the wind howled, and beat, and tore at the traffic light above Middle Street.

Chapter Two

Tight-Fast

Two things woke Gennis—the sunlight that hurt her eyes and the sound of Paunch's voice that hurt her ears.

"Gennis, I am hungry. Gennis, wake up," Paunch said right in her ear, shaking Gennis' shoulder.

"Me too, me too," Jolly said, pinfeathers poking out of her soppy hair.

Their home hung stone-still in the sky—at last. They stretched, yawned, and looked down from their nest ledge to see their mother's loom, with its banana spider silk weaving, broken and tumbled about. Delicate, pink seashell bowls, spider silk clothes, and all their quick-grass bread lay in a soggy jumble. The nest was a shambles and lone-stark because of the wild-salt-zebra-wind, and because their parentlings still had not returned. Yet the wind had stopped its terrible tantrum and they were tight-fast inside the nest.

"Motherly will not be glad-happy to see this mess and Fathling's new fishnet wrecked," Jolly said.

Paunch's stomach rumbled as he said, "Let us look for something to eat."

Gennis agreed. Gennis was only five-ish months old, but she knew that some things come firstly and some things come secondly. For now, it was food and water—firstly.

The nestlings stood up, stretched some more, and shook themselves dry like puppies. They peered under smashed bits and pieces of crockery, cups, and baskets. They rustled through the acorn shell cupboards. But it was no use, all the loaves, seeds, and elfin cake tasted like the saltly wind and rain.

They searched for a long time, trying to stack and sort as best as they could, but the day crept by without anything to eat, and worse, without any word from their motherly or their fathling. They searched for food and waited. They stacked broken dishes, squeezed out dripping bedding, and waited. They wondered, worried, and waited.

Late in the day, when Gennis noticed Paunch chewing contently, she wondered what he could have possibly found to eat that hadn't been ruined by the saltly water. "What have you found to eat, Paunch?"

"Nothing."

"Then what are you chewing?"

"I am not chewing." His cheeks bounced as he chewed.

"Paunch, this is no time for riddles or joking." Gennis tapped her toe.

"I am still very hungry," Jolly said. Jolly had finally found a small jug of mouse milk, but it had not gone far. Jolly's stomach had been talking to her for a long time now.

"Paunch, all the food is mushly and ruined. If you have found something to eat, Motherly would want you to share."

Paunch looked thunderstruck and said, "I have not found anything to eat, Gennis. I would share if I had." He continued chewing.

"But you are chewing."

"No, I am not, Gennis, I am just exercising my teeth on the air inside my mouth."

Gennis tapped her toe faster and said, "No jokes, Paunch. I do not know if you have noticed, but we have some worry-concern here."

"Paunch, Gennis is right. There is nothing goodly to eat in the nest, and we cannot fly," Jolly said, trying not to look too smartly as she spoke. Jolly liked to be right and make big important statements.

"We are fast-trapped," Jolly said.

"Of course we cannot fly. We are only five-ish months old," Paunch said.

Gennis pointed to the bottom of the nest, "Paunch, it is going to be sleep-dark soon."

They could all see how the sun had shifted, sending shadows stabbing across the opening in the bottom of the traffic light.

"Gennis," Jolly asked with a shudder, "do you think you will be able to use your gifting magic and make fairy lights for us tonight so that the nest is not so darkly?"

"I tried, but I am afraid I am not very good at it yet. I am sorry," Gennis said.

Gennis had just discovered that her gifting magic was to be able to make fairy lights with her hands. Of course, all pocket fairies have to work hard to find out what their special gifting magic is and how best to use it, and Gennis was no exception. And even though Gennis was good at another kind of magic—dedicated determination—which meant that she was good at not quitting or giving up, she was still just learning and couldn't always make her charmly magic work every time.

Jolly nodded her head, patted Gennis on the back, and understood. Jolly was still waiting to find out what her gifting magic might be, but so far it seemed Jolly's only special knack-gifts were being able to wiggle her ears, roll her tongue like a caterpillar, and please her parentlings. Jolly wanted very badly to do some silvery magic to help her family, especially now, with the sleep-dark creeping closer.

Paunch said, still pretending to chew, "Do not worry; Motherly and Fathling will be here soon. They will make lights for us."

Gennis tried to be patient and comforting like their motherly, but she wasn't very good at it. "Paunch, what are we going to do if Motherly does not come back tonight?"

Jolly's voice was very squeaky because Jolly always sounded squeakly when she had worry-concern. Jolly squeaked, "We are going to stay tight-fast in the nest—right, Paunch?"

"Yes," Paunch said and stopped pretend-chewing.

"That is what Motherly said to do, right, Paunch?" Jolly squeaked again.

"Yes," Paunch said, "and Fathling would want us to stay tight-fast in the nest too."

Gennis sounded less than comforting, "I know what our motherly said, but we need food and water, and what if they do not . . . ?"

Jolly squeaked louder, "Do not say it Gennis. Please do not. It cannot be true if you do not say it."

"Say what, Jolly?" Paunch sometimes had trouble following the sisterly talk.

"Please, do not, Gennis"

Paunch asked, "What?"

The light continued to slide away and the nest felt darkly and sad.

"What if what, Gennis? Jolly, is it a riddle?" Paunch demanded. He did not like being left out of any riddle telling.

"We are very tired, Paunch. Jolly and I are just teasing. Tomorrow Motherly and Fathling will come home. It is nothing to talk about now, Paunch. Jolly is right. It is nothing. Do not worry, Jolly, I will not say it tonight."

The nestlings bundled together, pulling the stick-bits of their ruined nest around them. Paunch's stomach rumbled low. Jolly whimpered a little in her sleep, and Gennis lay awake, hoping to hear the comforting whir of pocket fairy wings.

Chapter Three

Deciding to Decide

The next morning, dust drifting on bright streamers of light trickled into the pocket fairy nest above Middle Street. While Gennis squinted in the glare and tried smoothing the wrinkles out of the yellow stripes of her skirt, her stomach groan-growled. Paunch's hair was flat-mashed on the right side of his head but stuck out in wild spikes on the left side. He yawned and scratched the rosy tip of one ear, and straightened his red vest over his groan-moaning stomach. Jolly's fingers caught in a rat's nest tangle of hair. She frowned, thinking about trying to comb out the snarl without Motherly's help. Jolly's stomach groan-squeaked.

Gennis looked at her brotherling and sisterly and knew that their situation was much more serious than wrinkled skirts and snarlish hair. Their situation bordered on grim-dark. If they left the nest they would be disobeying Motherly. If they stayed too long without food and water, they would not live long enough to grow wings.

"Paunch, do you think that you could talk to the dust motes and find out if they know where our motherly and fathling might be?"

Paunch's gifting magic was to be able to talk to the specks of dust that danced through secret cracks into the traffic light. This proved a handy kind of magic because dust motes can be well traveled, and they are full of bits of interesting news, information, and stories that pocket fairies love. Dust motes and their cousins, fly specks, are famous for congregating here and there in billowy heaps. They rest quietly,

listening and remembering, until a
breath of wind or breeze sends them
rushing through space to some new
listening place. Dust mote bantering is
a rare gifting magic for pocket fairies,
but often a useful one.

"I will try, Gennis, but I have not
practiced my word-learning for a
while," Paunch said.

He began to whisper as the dust
motes floated closer to his face. Gennis
and Jolly waited as Paunch tipped his
head to listen to the floating flecks
darting in the air.

Paunch turned to his sisterlys and
frowned, "The dust motes are all
confused because of the wild-salt-zebra-wind, Gennis. Everyone is
mixed up and stirred together. One dust mote said that he could tell
me where to find the ocean of the merfolk, and another said that she
could tell me what the great river of grass is like far to the southly. But
none have heard anything about Motherly or Fathling. They will look
and see. And they will tell it when they have something to say. They
would be happy to do it."

The dust dropped away from Paunch, streaming down through the
opening in the bottom of the nest.

"Thank you for trying, Paunch," Gennis said. Her voice sounded
dry and croakly when she added, "Listen to me, both of you. Motherly
and Fathling may not be able to get back to us for a while, and they
will not be happy to find us tight-fast but all dried up in this nest."

Jolly wiped a hand across her pinkly nose and sniffed, and Paunch's
stomach grumbled again as he jumped down to the bottom of the nest
to watch the dust motes trail away.

Paunch, his face glum, asked, "But, Gennis, how can we leave the
nest? We still cannot fly. I checked this morning. We do not even have
wing buds yet. We would be excellent fall-downs, though."

"Listen," Gennis said, excitement in her voice, "I stayed awake
in the sleep-dark, and tried remembering. I remembered the story

Fathling told us about the nestlings of the Oberlin fairy clan and how the terrible-spotted-skin-grabbers had carried most of them back to their dankly-deep den, and there was no way they could escape by flying because their wings had not grown, either. So the nestlings thought about making a ladder from pine straw, and . . . ."

"And quick-grass," Paunch added.

"And quick-grass," Gennis repeated.

"And they all climbed out of the dankly-deep den," Jolly said.

"And they all climbed out of the dankly-deep den. We cannot fly, but we can try climbing down," Gennis said.

Paunch leaned farther over the edge of the nest opening. "Motherly would not like this, Gennis," he said, brightening a great deal at the thought of doing something as daring and desperate as the Oberlin fairy clan nestlings.

"We do not know what Motherly would think. We must do the thinking now."

Jolly sniffed one more time, grew quiet, and then said, "I will help you think, Gennis."

"Jolly, thank you," Gennis said, trying again to sound more like Motherly. "We are quick-smart nestlings. We can think a way out. We *will* think a way out."

Paunch lay flat on his tummy with most of his head hanging out of the nest. He had tried to make both sides of his hair match but one side still hung limp over his right eye. Impatiently, Paunch flipped his hair out of his face. His voice floated up to the ledge where Jolly and Gennis sat.

"Come and think with me down here," he said.

They jumped down next to Paunch and peered for the first time at what the wild-salt-zebra-wind had done to the world outside. The nestlings had never been out of their tight-fast nest, not even to practice wind balancing with their fathling. All they knew of the world was what their fathling had told them in stories and what they could see from the bottom of their nest in the sky. Some of what they saw, when they looked down, they thought they recognized. But to three know-not fairy nestlings, some of what they saw was part of the much bigger puzzle that was the wide-big world of Middleburg and beyond.

One thing they noticed was that the wild-salt-zebra-wind had left a bigger mess outside their nest than inside. Torn branches and trees lay in a tumble everywhere they looked. Pieces ripped from the pockling world rested beneath them in a great, tangled heap. The wind had blown part of a peaked roof with a running horse weathervane completely off its barn. The roof rested just beneath them and jutted up close to their nest, the metal horse spinning around and around. Pockling sounds and mysterious pockling magic, like chain saws and hammers, hummed and banged in the distance, but Gennis, Paunch, and Jolly did not have names for what they heard and for only a little of what they saw.

Of course what the nestlings saw was an upside down place, and it was hard to recognize even familiar things. One thing they did recognize, even from so high a place, was the leaping sparkle of light in a puddle of water. They licked their dry lips. Next to the puddle lay a branch full of elderberries. Those berries looked fat, black, and tart.

They rubbed their empty middles. They looked at each other. They were very hungry now. Paunch's stomach rumbled, then Jolly's stomach groaned, and Gennis' stomach rumbled and then groaned. They thought hard about pine straw ladders, daring escapes, cool sips of water, plump elderberries, and of course, strange pockling noises without names.

Mostly though, they tried to imagine ways to fly without wings.

Chapter Four

Hanging by a Banana Spider's Thread

Are those trees, Gennis? I thought that the trees would be more straight-tall," Jolly asked, her head in her hands, as they continued to stare down at Middleburg. Jolly pointed to a tangle of torn tree branches below them, leaves fluttering. Paunch wrinkled his nose, thinking. His head hung the farthest over the edge of the traffic light. They all lay flat on their stomachs, their swinging legs bent backward at the knees. Gennis bit her lip, trying to make their fathling's word-picture of trees match the sad pile of green leaves beneath them.

They had heard about the ancient cypress trees that stand sentinel in the Waverly Woods, the high-mile sailing clouds that skitter across the Purple Moon, and the Glitter Lakes where all deep thoughts go to wait for their owners' dreams, but none of them had ever seen the sky, or the moon in the sky, or a tree in a forest—or a tree, for that matter.

"Like Motherly's loom, I think the wild-salt-zebra-wind was not go-easy on the trees, Jolly." Gennis gestured to their motherly's loom. The loom lay next to Jolly in a wet pile of splintered wood and bedraggled yellow spider silk. Middleburg's trees lay in a wet tumble of shattered splinters below them.

Paunch wondered, "Where are the rusher-rumble-bys?"

Usually the orderly grey asphalt below them was filled with the din of pocklings in their rusher-rumble-bys. All day and night the rumble-bys

honked, beeped, chugged, squealed, and hummed along underneath the traffic light. Once in a while, two pocklings would crash their rumble-bys into each other with the jangle-screech of bending metal and the wail of honk-horns.

Sometimes it was exciting for the nestlings when two rusher-rumble-bys crashed, because their pockling rider-drivers would jump out shouting and waving at each other with hard looks and hard words. Sometimes it was sadly when a pockling was too bruised to yell or shout, and the nestlings would always make a well-wish for the bruised or the wounded.

Gennis, Paunch, and Jolly spent many sleep-slow afternoons counting the spinning wheels and gleamly metal hoods that flashed by beneath them. It was one of Paunch's favorite games to count the rumble-bys, and they all loved to play wish-games and wonder-dream about the endless places the pocklings raced to, but that was before the wild-salt-zebra-wind.

"Maybe too many stick-bits are in the way, Paunch, for the rusher-rumble-bys," Jolly offered.

After a moment Paunch admitted sadly, "I still do not have any bigly thoughts."

Gennis said, "That is all right. I do not either. Just do not stop trying, Paunch."

The day was so brightly that the nestlings had to squint against the light outside. They could hear wood splintering nearby. A sound like a swarm of quarreling bees whined in the distance. A drum-thumping noise pounded close.

Paunch wriggled around the opening trying to see what all the pockling noise was about. He jostled Jolly, who bumped into the pile of tumbled fishnet their motherly had been weaving. Jolly frowned at her brotherling and stood up, pulling and wrestling her motherly's loom out of the way. Stopping, her hands full of banana spider's silk, and her eyes wide with a sharp-smart idea, Jolly smiled.

Paunch said, "I am sorry to bump you, Jolly."

"No, do not be sorry. I want to say that you should have bumped me sooner," she said and laughed. "Will this help, Gennis?"

Making a wit-grin face at his youngest sisterly, Paunch said, "Of course that would help. It would help if the wild-salt-zebra-wind had filled the wide-big world with water all the way to the middle of Middleburg, so that we could let Fathling's fishnet down and catch fish right here from the nest. Or maybe we could train the fish to jump right into our nest and not bother to go fishing at all."

He sounded more dreamly than scornful when he said this last part, enjoying the pleasant vision of fish trained to jump right into their nest. Paunch could almost count them. He could certainly taste them.

Ignoring Paunch, Gennis glanced up. "Jolly, you are a bright-flyer. Paunch, what if we hang Fathling's net from the edge of the nest and then let the rest hang down? We can jump to that . . . that, um . . . uh, that spinning-horse-mountain-twirly-top. It will make an excellent climb-down," she said, pointing to the barn roof.

A gentle puff of breeze made the weathervane spin faster. Gennis had concluded that anything that tall and point-sharp must be a mountain. Wasn't it just like the mountain of the red bearded hobgoblins that Fathling had told them about?

"We could jump and miss," Paunch said, wanting to sound bravely, but the thought of actually leaving the nest made the ground seem a lot farther away than it had ever seemed before. Then he thought better of his comment, and not wanting his sisterlys to think that he was shake-afraid said, "Well, you two might jump and miss, but I will jump and land, and I will land right on that mountain horse and ride it." Paunch added the last boast as the weather vane twisted to a stop.

"And I will jump and land," Jolly said, thinking that Paunch sounded boastful and remembering his silly comment about fish trained to jump right into the nest. "But maybe I will not go for a ride today on the twirly-top-horse."

Gennis said, "Jolly and I can jump and land if you can. The net will let us down close enough. I think we can be as bravely as any Oberlin fairy nestlings."

They wrestled and tugged the fishing net closer to the opening so they could tie one side to a rusty bolt. With a count of three-ish and a good, solid kick, Paunch, Jolly, and Gennis shoved the half-finished fishnet over the edge of the nest. The wooden top of the loom held tight on the bolt. The bulk of the net hung like a ladder in the air, swaying back and forth in the same breeze that made the weather vane spin. The three were pleased to see how close the bottom of the fishnet hung to the top of what Gennis called their twirly-top-mountain.

Paunch, who liked to worry about such things as firstly and lastly, asked, "Who will climb down firstly?"

I will go," Gennis said, "and then Jolly, and if anything happens, because you are stronger, you can pull us up."

Paunch smiled, thinking Gennis was being very nice to mention his rock-strong strength. Actually, Gennis was worried that Paunch would get silly, forget what he was doing, and tumble off the fishnet.

Jolly pulled a lantana bloom from a bouquet she had found under an acorn water dipper. She shoved the yellow flower into the snarl in her hair. Jolly shrugged at Gennis' frown and said, "I won't go into the wide-big world looking grub-rumpled."

Gennis shook her head and backed out of the nest and started climbing down the net by putting her feet carefully on her motherly's tight weaving. Jolly followed and the fishnet shook a little. The sun glowed warm on the backs of their hands, and the breeze sang in their ears through the netting. Like spiders in a web, the nestlings could feel each other's smallest movements—little shake-trembles as the fishnet swayed.

"You are so very close to the top of the twirly-top-mountain, Gennis," Paunch called, sounding thrilled.

Distracted, Gennis looked up at her brotherling. Her foot plunged through the open weaving as she slipped and the net shook. Jolly froze, clinging tight. Gennis grabbed spider silk.

Paunch yelled down helpfully, "Maybe you should not look up while you are climbing down."

"Maybe you should not distract me." Gennis pulled herself up, carefully placing her foot back on the sharp-bright, yellow silk. With her hand wrapped in the netting she looked down again. The twirly-top-mountain *was* very close, just as Paunch had said, and she thought it would not take too great a leap for her to land on it. She started to count to ten-ish. Ten-ish always seemed a goodly number to count to when Gennis was looking for her bravely heart.

She had just started to say four-ish when her whole world (beneath, below, and around) started to shake, reel, and tumble out of control.

Under her hands and feet the fishnet jumped like a cricket gone sun-silly. Gennis could hear Jolly, squeaking and hiccupping, as a rumbling, snorting roar thundered through the air all around them. She heard Paunch yelp.

Horrified, Gennis felt the fishnet start to unravel beneath her hands. The huge, snorting, shaking rattle was pulling the net apart, and Nanda's carefully woven loops fell away, one after another. Gennis grabbed at a single strand of silk.

"Tight-hold!" someone yelled. The fishnet unraveled like the hem of an old cloak through their hands. Gennis grabbed tighter and tighter until her hands ached.

Suddenly a cloud of chokely smoke poured over her in a rush. Even in the darkness of the smoke, Gennis could feel the mad rumble-shake all around her, and her ears were filled with a new sound—a screaming whistle. And then following the smoke came another cloud, this time of dustly dirt that made Gennis cough.

When the rumble-down and whistling stopped, Gennis dared to look around. Like real spiders dangling from a real wisp of spider's web, the three nestlings clung to a single glistening strand of silk. Somehow, Paunch had managed to end upside down, tangled in what was left of the fishnet by one foot. He hung just above Jolly.

Hanging upside down made Paunch's shirt and mouse leather vest peel down his body and bunch up around his neck. It looked like his clothes were trying to crawl over his head and get away. Jolly had her hands and feet wrapped so tightly in the spider silk she looked like she was growing from it. The yellow silk cut across her pale muslin gown crushing the flower petals Motherly had sewn to the front. Dirt had turned Gennis' yellow striped skirt to a muddly brown. She sneezed.

When Gennis looked down, she gasped, and then she gulped, because somehow in all that roaring, rattling, black tumble-shake, their mountain climb-down had been swept away. The twirly-top-mountain had disappeared like a handful of sparks, and so had the trees and the storm rubble; even the elderberries were gone. Middle Street had been swept clean as if by a giant's sweeply broom. The road below them was empty, and there was no place left for three dare-great nestlings to jump.

Chapter Five

Costard

"Pull . . . us . . . up, Paunch," Gennis choked, wanting to be mistaken, hoping she was wrongly, when she thought about Paunch falling out of the nest. "Paunch brotherling, pull us up."

Jolly squeaked, "Help!" Gennis could feel the silk tremble in her hands; Jolly's shivers were making it shake.

"Tight-squeeze, Jolly," Gennis said as she tight-squeezed. She could feel her own shaking start. A small quake of fear rolled down from her shoulder and crawled right out to her fingers. "Tight-squeeze, Gennis," she whispered to herself.

She put her head back and yelled, "Paunch!" A whistle roared over the stranded nestlings, and Gennis thought she was about to be eaten by the monsterly that seemed to be eating everything else. "Can you see the monsterly, Paunch?"

"There is a monsterly, too?" Paunch sounded more interested than worry-concerned.

"It must be a monsterly. Something dreadful made us shake apart and almost fall," Jolly said.

"I see it, Gennis. I see it!" Paunch yelled as another burst of noise and shaking sent the nestlings twirling around, and now the sisterlys could see it too.

"Yes, that is a monsterly," Paunch sounded cheer-bright, "but it is going away, I think."

"It is as big as a Drizzle Mountain leprechaun, but all yellow," Jolly described. The monsterly burped smoke and shrieked another ear-splitting whistle.

"The monsterly just burped smoke. It is . . . a dragon," Paunch breathed. "Could it be a dragon, Gennis?" Paunch was beginning to sound delighted.

Gennis could see that the monsterly had a huge mouth shaped like a bucket, full of snarl-sharp teeth. It was trying to eat all the trees left from the storm, and was pushing them about with its toothly mouth.

"It is going away," Jolly confirmed, "and so is our only way to climb down from here."

Gennis could see the twirly-top-horse, the mountain, and everything that had been underneath them trapped in the monsterly's enormous teeth. Gennis' heart jumped funny in her chest, and she said half heartedly, "Paunch, pull us up."

"I will, Gennis, just as . . ."

"Good brotherling."

". . . soon as someone pulls me up."

When she tipped her head all the way back, Gennis could see Paunch dangling above Jolly. Paunch was still upside down. Paunch caught Gennis' eye, and incredibly, he waved. She laughed.

"Well Gennis, we are in some trouble-bother now, I think. I am only hanging up here by one foot," he observed.

Before he could start to annoy her, she asked him, "Can you not pull yourself up?"

"Uhmmm, no, I cannot."

"Gennis, I am very shakely."

"I know Jolly. Why don't you think up another bright-flyer idea for us?"

"But look what happened to us after the last bright-flyer idea."

Paunch yelled down to his sisterlys, "You know what Motherly says. This is just chance-luck. Think hard, Jolly. My head is sloshing."

Paunch's face was turning a funny shade of red. Gennis said, "We need a huge-big-hero-great-slay-the-dragon-save-the-nestlings idea."

"Are you thinking too, Gennis?" Paunch wasted time asking.

She was just about to tell Paunch to be quiet and think harder when the spider silk in her shake-sweat hands swung away from her in a golden arc. The silken thread flew up and away across the sky until the three nestlings were swinging, their hands gripped tight and their feet dangling, except for Paunch, who dangled by one foot, like fish caught on their fathling's stringer.

Gennis could hear Jolly chanting over and over at the top of her lungs, "Hang on! Hang on! Hang on!" Gennis thought that it was good advice now that chance-luck seemed to be in charge again.

Paunch yelled, "Oh greatly goodness."

In a moment, Gennis felt herself gently lowered to the roof of their very own nest. The metal top of the traffic light felt firm-steady under her shakely feet and legs.

"First birdling, second birdling, and . . . ." Paunch landed with a plop on his hands and knees. " . . . third birdling. If thou wert trying to fly, thou shouldest try letting go of thy rope," a trim, gray bird announced after dropping the spider silk.

"I wast but fixing my nest after the big wet howl of wind last night, when I thought, 'twas a lovely bit of yellow thread that thou wast clinging to and wouldest make a lovely nest trim."

Ignoring the bird, Gennis scrambled to Jolly, who was still clutching the spider silk and muttering, "The world is too wide-big. The world is too wide-big. The world is . . . ."

Jolly clutched at Gennis, the bedraggled yellow flower hanging over her left eye, and said, "We are too bit-small."

"Thought 'twas pretty, this bit of thread. I did not notice the birdlings until, well, I looketh more closely."

Pausing to look around and commenting on their vantage point from the top of the traffic light the bird quoted, "'When lofty trees I see barren of leaves.'"

This comment about their surroundings turned the nestling's attention away from their near disaster to their marvelous luck-joy. Jolly and Gennis helped Paunch to his feet, and as they steadied themselves, their eyes grew huge. The world was indeed wide-big. Jolly was right.

The sky filled all the space above their heads and all the space around their nest. They were swimming in sky. The green earth stretched away and filled all the corners beneath them. In a field across the road from them, the yellow smoke-burping monsterly pushed trees and trash here and there into heaps—saving them for later to eat, probably. The nestlings looked at each other and thought to themselves, where in all this bigly space could their motherly and fathling possibly be?

Paunch spoke for each of them when he whispered, "Where are they?"

Their luck-true friend hopped onto a thick cable next to them and tipped his head at them. Their nest hung from a cable which ran from their home in the traffic light to poles on opposite sides of the intersection. Below them, on one corner, was a pockling nest with the words, *Gas-N-Go*, but the store's neon sign was dark and its doors locked. Stick-bits littered the parking lot. Someone would have to come clean up all the rubbish from the wild-salt-zebra-wind. The nestlings hoped it wouldn't be the yellow monsterly.

Gennis pointed. In the corner of the *Gas-N-Go* parking lot they could see a white flesh-scratcher slinking near a dumpster, its tail bent and nubby. They looked at each other. Seeing the flesh-scratcher gave the nestlings a funny lump in their throats. The world was not only wide-big, it was also filled with many carve-sharp dangers.

Their bird deliverer watched them watching Middleburg, his head tipping from side to side. The fresh breeze ruffled the sleek feathers of his head. He waited patiently for them to finish their astonished looking.

Finally, he spoke.

"Thou art not birdlings?" he asked.

"No, we are pocket fairies. My brotherling is Paunch, my sisterly is Jolly, and my name is Gennis."

"No, thou art not birdlings. I see that now. And I am Costard."

"Costard," Gennis repeated, "you are our luck-true hero."

Costard plumped himself, shook his head, and replied modestly, "It was a mere accident of fortuitous fortune, only."

"Well, we would be much closer to the hard-downly ground if you had not helped us," Paunch said, sidling up to Costard. Since Paunch had recently been hanging upside down looking at too much of the ground for his taste, he felt particularly warm-true towards their unexpected rescuer.

"Wast thou trying to fly, small wingless one?" Costard stretched one delicate claw out and scratched his head. Paunch tried to stretch like Costard and scratch his own head with his foot and almost toppled over backwards.

Jolly answered for all of them, "No, we were not trying to fly, not at all. We have lost our motherly and fathling and are hungry and thirsty and we almost fell downly, aaaand . . . !" Jolly's voice broke and became a whine, then a wail. Then she started to hiccup. Gennis and Paunch put their arms around Jolly and hoped she would stop before they all started to eye-leak.

In a singsong voice Costard mimicked Jolly's voice, "No, we were not trying to fly, not at all. We have lost our motherly and fathling and are hungry and thirsty, and we almost fell downly, aaaand . . . !" He mimicked her crying right down to the hiccups.

Costard the bird said, "A most dark turn of fate's winds, assuredly."

Jolly, startled at the unexpected performance, turned to Gennis and asked, "Is that what I sound like?"

Gennis laughed and clapped. The imitation was so perfect that Jolly had forgotten to cry.

"You are a mockingbird," Gennis said, delighted.

"Thou art a bright wingless one," Costard said. He blinked his eyes at Gennis, observing her closely, and continued, "'For I have sworn thee fair, and thought thee bright.'"

"Thank you," Gennis said, blushing. Paunch snickered and Jolly continued to forget to remember to cry.

"It is not original with me, thou shouldest know. Thou shouldest also know that I have ever been one to do what I can for those who are 'frantic-mad with evermore unrest.'"

Paunch yawned.

Costard looked at the yawning Paunch and said, "Perhaps that one is less than 'frantic-mad.' Nevertheless, I shall befriend thee. Wait upon my return. I bid thee, anon."

And with a flurry of feathers, Costard the mockingbird flew away.

Chapter Six

A Maybe False Friend

Jolly watched Costard fly away. "Our new friend is some rise-higher flyer, isn't he Gennis?" she said wistfully.

Gennis nodded. She was still feeling a tickle in her stomach from so much big-sky around and she jumped when Paunch shouted her name.

"Gennis, Jolly, we do not have to be born flyers if we follow this sky-path," Paunch said and pointed.

Not waiting for an answer or even his sisterly's full attention, Paunch skipped along the thick, black cable running from the traffic light to the tall poles standing like sentinels on opposite sides of Middle Street.

"Look, Jolly, how easy. We can get down from here. No climbing or falling."

Paunch skipped all the way to the top of one pole, turned around, backed up, and started to slide backwards down a taut, thick wire that ran from the top of the pole down to the ground.

"Wait, Paunch, go slow. Look-watch," Gennis warned.

Both sisterlys scrambled to catch the exuberant Paunch, but before they could reach the top of the pole, he was halfway down the wire.

"Maybe you should wait for Costard? Maybe you should?" Jolly yelled and pointed to the empty sky while racing after Gennis to the top of the straightly pole.

Their brotherling laughed as he slid down backwards. He laughed and laughed until he hit a plastic yellow label full of pockling words: Warning, Danger, High Voltage!

"Ooof, I am slow-stuck."

"Be still, Paunch. We should be careful of being seen."

"The wild-salt-zebra-wind has blown everyone away, Gennis."

"Not everyone, you wit-nit, we are still here, and I hope you do not think Motherly and Fathling are blown away." Gennis could feel a familiar impatience crawl up her neck.

"Be still. Pocklings may be about. That noisy, tree-eating monsterly was controlled by pockling magic. I feel it."

Gennis turned to slide down to Paunch, when out of the corner of her quickly eye she noticed the switching tail of a whisker-licking flesh-scratcher. She recognized that it was a flesh-scratcher right away. Fathling had described their whiskery faces full of cunning smiles, mewling meows, and sharply teeth. He had talked of their unblinking eyes that glow green or yellow in the night. And she knew that pocket fairies were a favorite for their scratching claws.

The flesh-scratcher moved again. It was threading its way from behind the dumpster, through a jumble of tree branches, right towards them.

"Do not move, Paunch. A flesh-scratcher is right beneath you," Gennis said, trying to sound strong and commanding for her brotherling's sake, but the sight of the flesh-scratcher with its twitchly tail had made the big-sky tickle in her stomach worse.

She said, "I think that it may be waiting for you to fall."

"Go away. We see you," Jolly hollered, jumping up and down on top of the pole, waving her arms.

The flesh-scratcher crept forward and plopped down under the now cling-tight Paunch. It smiled with a sharply grin. Paunch's eyes were as round as two moons in still water.

In a raspy voice, the flesh-scratcher, its white fur matted and caked with mud, called up to the nestlings, "You are young to be leaving a safe nest, my little friends. It's all right, young ones. My name is Feral, and I am certainly here to be of some help, I think."

Feral's bent tail twitched, thump—thump. Feral the flesh-scratcher slicked his paw and wiped a bit of drool from his chin. The sight of the plump, fresh, fairy nestling sitting just out of his reach made his mouth driply. He cleared his throat to disguise the deep rumbling of his empty stomach.

Paunch yelled up to his sisterlys, "He says that he is a friend, Gennis."

"Do not move, Paunch," Gennis commanded.

"That is good advice from your sisterly. You are somewhat high up," Feral said with another slow slick of one paw. "I am thinking that, perhaps, you are Marker and Nanda's nestlings."

In surprise Paunch sat straight up. He yelled, "He knows our parentlings!"

"What do you know of Marker Best Moon and Nanda Star Shimmer?" Jolly demanded, shocked.

"I know that they chose well in choosing that nest of yours in the sky. I know that they are quick-smart, and . . ." Feral said, pausing, ". . . and I know where they might be right now." The muddy tail, full of burrs, continued thumping.

"Gennis, did you hear what Feral has said about our motherly and fathling? He does know them. He says that they are quick-smart, and they are. He says that they are good choosers, and they are. And he says he knows where they are right now," Paunch called up in a delighted voice,

clapping his hands. Then he waved to Gennis and Jolly, but his happy waving made Paunch forget to be tight-steady. He started to wobble, just a bit at first, and then a bit more.

When Feral the flesh-scratcher sat up and gave the wire a shake with one muckly paw, Paunch lost his balance completely. Tipping over with a yelp, Paunch wound up swinging by his hands and knees. He was hanging from the wire the way that an apple or an orange hangs from a tree branch.

"Gennis," he reported in a breathless voice, "I am upside down, again."

"Drop down little one, and I will catch you," Feral said, his voice rasping friendly and encouraging.

"Oh, Paunch, you silly nestling, Feral is no true-friend. You should not have been jack-legging. He did not say that he knows. He said that he *might* know where our motherly and fathling are. You should hear with better ears, Paunch," Jolly shouted down to her brotherling.

"Come now. Do not fear. The fall is not as far as I first thought."

Feral's tail thumped faster.

"I cannot hold on ever-long. Gennis, perhaps I should drop down."

"You hold on. Tight-hold! I am coming down." Gennis turned to slide down the silvery wire. "Do not listen to this maybe false friend," she yelled down. "If he is a true friend then he will tell us right now where our motherly and fathling are—if he even knows."

Feral gave the wire another shake while Gennis' back was turned.

Jolly shouted, "He is no fast-true friend, Gennis. I saw that flesh-scratcher shake the wire and try to make Paunch drop off."

"If my sisterly says you are false, then you are false," Gennis yelled.

"Gennis, my face is red again," Paunch said.

Feral said, "Would a false friend give you such important news?"

"If you are true, then say where they are," Gennis said, trying not to slide too fast and shake both herself and Paunch off of the wire.

Feral's voice cajoled, "They are very near to here. Come down and I will show you." Pocket fairies could be very taste-tender; Feral remembered as he swiped drool from his mouth with a paw.

"You are just saying that so you can tear us and eat us," Jolly yelled at Feral while Gennis slid closer to Paunch.

"Where is our motherly?" Paunch said, but his voice sounded tired.

"Where is our fathling?" Jolly used her most sternly voice.

"Come, Paunch, and let me catch you. You are very tired, I can tell," Feral said, ignoring their questions.

Feral's tail thumped faster and faster.

"He is right, Gennis, my hands are going to slip."

Too excited to be patient, Feral sat up on his hind legs and grinned, his teeth glint-bright in the sun. Gennis, who had turned to see how close she was to Paunch, gasped, when she saw the sharpness of that smile beneath them.

"I will pull you up." Gennis reached down to Paunch. His face was purple now.

Jolly screamed, "There is another flesh-scratcher, Paunch, and another!"

Gennis did not look down into the sudden, swirling mob of teeth and tails. She could hear the meowing, hissing growls beneath them. The flesh-scratchers had come creeping from behind the *Gas-N-Go* dumpster, crawling from under trashcans, and slinking from beneath a scraggly hedge. Reaching for Paunch, she grabbed for his vest as he clenched his teeth against the pain in his hands and the sweat in his eyes.

"I am too tired."

"Now is when you must try ever-hard." Gennis tugged. Paunch tried. Jolly yelled and waved her arms.

"Go away! Go away!" she yelled.

Paunch gasped, "I'm falling."

"No, Paunch!" Gennis reached down and pulled at Paunch's vest with both hands, her legs wrapped tight to hold on. The wire bounced beneath them as one ragged flesh-scratcher after another jounced the base of the wire. Their meowing howls grew louder.

"I . . . will . . . not . . . let you fall!" Gennis shouted and yanked.

Gennis had just begun to think that she was not going to be able to hold them both steady on the bucking wire when there was a great rush of wings and a screeching holler from the sky. Costard the mockingbird dropped down to give a great stabbing peck to Feral's scruffy head. With his best impression of a bald eagle, Costard swooped up, climbed, and wheeled to dive bomb one flesh-scratcher after another.

Jolly whooped with surprise and relief, "Costard, you *are* a rise-higher flyer!"

Chapter Seven

A Pocket Full of Pocket Fairies

The flesh-scratchers growled, and their stomachs rumbled. Costard screeched. Jolly cheered for Costard. Gennis ordered Paunch to tight-hold. A noise as fierce and big as the wild-salt-zebra-wind filled the air.

Just as the noise grew to its growling, screeching, and cheering loudest, and just below the dangling Paunch, in the middle of the milling flesh-scratchers, rising right out of the ground like a giant mushroom popped the enormous head of a pockling. The hole was deep where he had been working to fix the lights of Nanda and Marker's sky-nest. And only the pockling's head stuck out of it.

The hole was deep, but not deep enough that the pockling hadn't heard the noise of seven howling flesh-scratchers, one sky-diving mockingbird, and three distraught fairy nestlings. When the pockling stood up to see what all the noise was about he was shocked by the sight of so many angry, mangy, flesh scratching alley cats. The storm had upset them he thought. They certainly looked upset—and hungry. Their lumpy ribs poked from skinny sides as they stalked by.

The flesh-scratchers ignored the pockling until he straightened up and waved a pair of wire cutters over his head at them. He shouted and waved.

He yelled, "Scat!"   He shook his wire cutters at them.

"Get!" he insisted.

It was hard for Feral's scraggly gang to drag their eyes away from the plump, delicious, dangling Paunch. But a shouting pockling head and a waving pockling hand shaking a magic wand at them was too much. And that stupid bird, Costard, who had flown away at the astounding appearance of the pockling, sat on a telephone pole, waiting to continue his foul attack. Feral gave Paunch one final, longing look and then he ran. His flesh-scratching gang followed. The pockling watched as they scurried away, back to the dumpster behind the *Gas-N-Go*.

To Gennis the pockling seemed as big as the sky because he was everywhere she looked. He took the magic wand and used it to scratch behind one sunburned ear as he watched the fleeing Feral. She was too fascinated by that vast-grand fist holding the wand to be afraid. The pockling's hair poked out like Paunch's, and it made Gennis think of motherly's broom-sweep. He was close enough to Paunch that Gennis could count the sun-speckles on his nose and wonder at the tightly weaving of his shirt.

Gennis wanted very much to shout out her thank-gladness for his wonderful pockling magic. He still held the strange wand in his hand. How impressed Gennis was that the pockling had used his magic to banish the flesh-scratchers and that sharp-toothed Feral. This digging-in-the-dirt pockling had saved Paunch and he had made the magic look ease-neat.

Before she could think what should come next, Paunch finally lost his grip on the sky-wire, gasping as he dropped. Tumbling like a dandelion seed, Paunch fell head first, luck-golden, into the pockling's leather pocket that he was wearing buckled tight around his enormous waist. Paunch, glad not to be flesh scratched or worse, scrambled onto a ball of twist-twine to peek over the edge of the tool belt and waved up at Gennis.

Gennis tried not to laugh or cry at her glee-glad-luckly brotherling. She shrugged her shoulders and not seeing any other choice-chance, and doubting that she could ever climb back up the sky-wire, jumped into the pockling pocket next to Paunch.

Jolly was so shocked by the sight of her brotherling and sisterly disappearing into the pocket of the towering digging-in-the-dirt pockling that all she could do was sit down—stunned—next to Costard.

Costard tried singing like a whippoorwill for Jolly. He tried hard to make her smile. He did not think she noticed.

"Gennis, it is very nice to be stuck in this hard-tight place with you," Paunch said pleasantly, smiling.

Gennis brushed herself off, smiled back at him,   and said, "Thank you."

The pocket shook and Paunch lost his grip on the edge of the tool belt. He and Gennis tumbled deeper into the pocket. The leather sides closed in tight around them as they struggled to their feet. A thin strip of sky glowed far above their heads, but down in the pocket bottom there were shadows and black corners.   Metal clinked. The air was thick-close and full of sharp smells, and every time the pockling moved Paunch and Gennis lost their balance and rolled deeper into the black bottom.

Gennis wanted very badly to tell Jolly not to have worry-concern, but Jolly was a problem as far above them as the clouds. Gennis could not even begin to imagine what to do about it. And Jolly was not her only puzzle-worry. Paunch and Gennis were safe from Feral the flesh-scratcher for now, but they were tight-trapped in a shadowy, shaky place far beneath the sky.

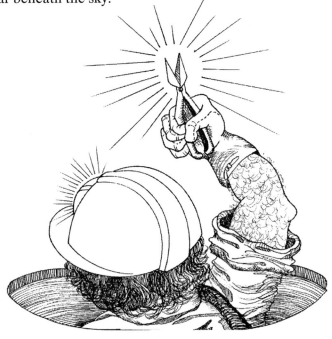

Chapter Eight

A Pockling Mile

I f it were not so trapped-tragic to be stuck in this darkly pocket, this would be an interesting place, Gennis." Paunch held up a curl of bright orange wire. "Look at this, Gennis. And this," Paunch said, kicking at a crackly twist of paper that smelled of lemon and sugar. Gennis could see Paunch's foot straight through the paper the same way she could see her own hand under water.

Paunch sounded out the word printed across the paper, "Caa . . . nnn . . . dy. Candy. Will not Fathling be proud to hear how good I am doing at pockling word learning? And dust-speak and bravely deeds and . . . ."

"Paunch, do not bother that. What if the pockling needs that?" Gennis whispered because she could hear the digging-in-the-dirt-pockling humming. Although she knew that even if he heard them he would never think to look for pocket fairies.

The tool belt vibrated with humming. The vibrations drummed beneath Gennis' feet and strummed in her head. Her nose was full of smells. The pockling candy paper smelled like motherly's lemon seed balm and the pocket smelled of mouse leather and rustly metal. She felt as if they were drowning in pockling smells and sounds. Gennis realized that her chest hurt from holding her breath.

Paunch had the good sense to look a little bit sheeply. "What are we going to do?"

Gennis took a deep breath and said, "We are going to be ready-bold-smart-keen pocket fairies. This is just a kind of pocket, after all, and we are clever nestlings."

Paunch scrambled to his feet. "If we climb up the side of this pockling ball of twist-twine," Paunch said, huffing as he climbed, "we can see out."

Paunch balanced on the top of the ball of twine and peeked over the edge of the pocket. He said, "You can see . . . hmmmm . . . a lot of dirt. But the sky is still up and the dirt is still down, and that is good. Do you think that this pockling lives in this dirtly hole in the ground?"

"Don't be silly, Paunch. Remember Fathling saying that pocklings live in giant nests called housely-homes that are full of nooks and crannies and pockets for folklings like us to live in. This pockling is obviously digging for something, maybe a trovely treasure. And a good thing for you, or you would be flesh scratched and . . . ."

"Shhh, Gennis, we should be thinking about brightly ways to get out of this pocket and not about Feral the false friend." For the first time Paunch sounded grumply.

He dropped back down next to Gennis. Paunch looked at her out of the corner of his eye and said, "What is your smartly idea?"

"I am thinking that," Gennis yelled, "you should hang on again." Everything in the tool belt shook, rattled, and shifted wildly. She braced herself against the sides of the tool belt.

Bits of wire jumped and tumbled about. A metal screw rolled by, barely missing Paunch's leg. The nestlings were jounced and jostled as the light inside the pocket grew brighter and sharper.

"The pockling is walking us somewhere. We are not in the darkly dirt any more," Paunch said.

"Where is he going? What if he does not stop soon, Paunch? He could walk a pockling mile, and unless we can learn to fly without wings we will never be able to get back to Jolly," Gennis said. She fell to one knee.

Gennis glanced at Paunch's white face. A pockling mile was as far as any pocket fairy with up-grown wings could ever imagine traveling. It seemed farther than the forest of the Oberlin fairy clan or the Rumble Down Hills.

"Come on, Paunch," Gennis said, pulling hard at a length of twine from the bottom of the tool belt. "We are done with this ride."

The nestlings wrestled their way past something called a *Measure It*, and the sharp end of a pointly tool shaped like one of motherly's javelins.

"You climb up, and I will hand you the twist-twine," Gennis said.

Paunch thought another climb-down on a dangling rope was the last thing he wanted, but Gennis wasn't going to be dragged a pockling mile from Jolly by this digging-in-the-dirt-pockling or any other. Paunch had to agree, so he climbed.

"The flesh-scratchers will not be around because they will still be shake-stiff because of this pockling's wand-magic," Paunch shouted from the top of a box with the words *Wire Nuts* on it.

"Catch this," Gennis said, tossing the twist-twine up to Paunch. Gennis made a good throw and Paunch made a good catch.

They tried to make it quick-fast work to catch the twine and push it over the edge of the tool belt, but every time the pockling took a step the tool belt shifted. Gennis and Paunch had to hang on with strong-fast hands. Twice, they were knocked to the bottom of the pocket by the jolting ride. Once, an enormous roll of slick, black stick-tape fell. It almost made Gennis into a smooth-flat nestling, but Gennis quick-crawled out of the way.

The pockling walked on and on. They felt that he had walked at least a pockling mile and maybe an inchly inch more when he finally stopped.

Paunch and Gennis were just edging over the side of the pocket when they heard a joyous voice above them. They looked up and were shocked to see Jolly. She was high above their heads—waving and calling.

"My beloved litter mates, forsooth, up here."

They could see Jolly just above the pockling's head. Tight-fast in an elegant bird's nest, she peered down over the edge at them from the *O* in the word *Go* in the sign *Gas–N–Go*.

"Costard brought me to his nest. It is tight-fast. He fed me elderberries and taught me to say words like 'beloved' and 'forsooth,'" Jolly called down as she waved a stalk of plump, black elderberries at Paunch and Gennis.

The pocket stopped shaking when the digging-in-the-dirt-pockling bent to fiddle with some wires on the wall of the *Gas–N–Go*. He never thought to check for pocket fairies in a bird's nest above his head, or pocket fairies in the tool belt around his waist. Reaching into his tool belt, he searched for his flat-head-twister-tool. Paunch gasped when that too big, searching hand almost grabbed up Gennis too. She scooted out of the way and pressed against the side of the pocket as the pockling's hand skimmed by.

"Come on," Gennis finally choked out.

She was too hungry and too tired to dodge any more giant crushing hands or to do any more big Oberlin fairy clan thinking. She was getting out. So she climbed onto that ball of twist-twine and then up the back of the blue work shirt with the words, *Middleburg Power and Light,* across it. She grabbed fistfuls of blue shirt and scrambled, climbing straight to the pockling's shoulder. Paunch gulped and followed.

The pockling felt a tickle now and again as the two nestlings clambered fast-quick up his shirt to his shoulder. But for pocklings, sometimes it is too much to imagine that fairy nestlings can be riding around in their tool belts, using their shirts as an escape, or waving elderberries in a bird's nest next to their heads. So, often they don't even look when they're tickled in silly places that make no sense by things that cannot be there. Finishing his check of the *Gas-N-Go,* the digging-in-the-dirt-pockling turned to walk a pockling mile back to his work in the hole next to Middle Street.

Just as he turned, Paunch and Gennis jumped. Paunch hadn't waited for any Oberlin fairy daring either. He had scrambled right after Gennis and straight to the enormous shoulder where Gennis pulled him up. With one strongly leap, Paunch and Gennis landed on top of a neatly trimmed hedge that grew along the wall of the *Gas-N-Go* building.

From there it was an easy jump to the bricks of the building. Then it was a nimble-quick climb along the grooves and cracks of the building. They climbed straight up to Costard's nest where Jolly and their supper waited.

"Mmmm, foodly," Paunch smiled, sighing and chewing.

Jolly laughed, hugged them both hard, and gave them each another berry while Paunch and Gennis laughed and hugged her back. It had been an adventurous morning for the three young pocket fairies, and they were delighted to have finally succeeded in accomplishing the first part of their search-quest—finding breakfast.

Chapter Nine

Costard's Nest

This is a lovely nest. Do you not think so, Gennis? I think so," Jolly said, leaning back against the braided twigs, a smear of elderberry juice across her mouth.

"Lovely," Gennis agreed, and it was lovely to feel close-safe and tight-fast again.

Costard had woven a neatly nest made of colorful bits and strips, and he had tucked it very cleverly into the big *O* in the *Gas-N-Go* sign where Jolly had been waiting for them.

From Costard's nest the nestlings could see their own sky-nest swinging high above Middle Street. They could hear an occasional snort from the still hungry, pushing monsterly with its bucket mouth, and they could watch for any pocklings who might appear or disappear in strange or unexplained ways.

Gennis ran her hands down the sides of the nest admiring Costard's workmanship. She could see the long strands of a horse's blonde tail and a bit of orange satin used as a hair pretty by some pockling sisterly. Costard had twisted long strips of yellowed paper covered with pockling words through the twigs and grass. Gennis smiled at the clever care behind Costard's workmanship.

When Costard coasted to a landing, Paunch said, "Why Costard, you've made a snuggly nest here. Thank you for your warmly welcome." Paunch wanted to show off his goodly manners even though elderberry juice dripped from his chin.

Costard perched on the nest's edge and observed the nestlings quietly. "May it please one and all, I am returned, and it rounds the eye to see this nest full of young, hungry nestlings," he remarked with a mournful sigh.

"Have you no nestlings?" Paunch asked.

"Not as yet." A tip of his head and a quick head scratch made Costard look a little sad. "So, it is good to have thy family here."

Paunch smiled and flopped onto his round-full belly and began reading the singing words written on the strips of paper woven throughout the nest, " 'Ever shall in safety rest. Trip away; Make no stay; Meet me all by break of day.' What does that mean?" Paunch wondered.

Costard tipped his head at the sound of Paunch's strong reading voice. Costard's eyes shone.

"'In safety rest' as it was in mine own egg nest. I have wished for a safe and fair place to rest and live, and I have constructed this nest with the sweet and singing tones of a great maker of fair words. My own sweetly matriarch and fond sire used these very words to build their birdlings a goodly nest and true from the pages of *The Complete Works of William Shakespeare*, a great maker of fair pockling words.

"It was a book left by some ruffian to rot in a dust bin behind this very pockling place." Costard tipped his head toward the *Gas-N-Go*. He shook his head, remembering. "My nest mates and I learned to mock and sing to the comedy and tragedy of that great book of ringing words."

"It is a wonderful egg nest," Jolly said, "and you should have nestlings."

"I agree; for this purpose I have created this nest. I see that thou doest approve?"

With their middles full of elderberries and a sweet feeling of safety in their hearts and minds, the nestlings approved completely. They could see that Costard would be a good fathling. Costard knew what nestlings needed—a tight nest and full stomachs.

"Oh, yes, we approve, and we think that you will find a sweetling soon," Jolly assured their newly friend.

"Be well, come and rest from overmuch fear, young pocket fairies of Middleburg. My nest is high and safe. Rest yourselves."

Turning to Jolly, Costard added, "Doest thou not have somewhat to say to thine family, Jolly the rise-higher flyer?"

Jolly's eyes lit up with Costard's reminder. "Oh, Gennis, how could I forget? I flew!" Her smile threatened to spill off the edges of her face. Happiness pinked her cheeks and made her forget that she hadn't combed her hair. "Costard flew me here on his back, Paunch! I flew!" Jolly sighed. Paunch smiled through the berry juice that dripped from his chin to his shirt front, and Gennis hugged Jolly. Costard ruffled his feathers and preened.

"Oh Jolly, you are the first one of us to fly. That is so brave-bright."

"Jolly was much distressed to see thee carried away by that pockling from the dirt. I couldest not leave her to such sad distress."

"Oh, good Costard, thank you for Jolly, and thank you, and thank you, and thank you again for this tight-fast place."

"Wouldest thou like some wriggling worms most juicy?' The bird inquired with dignity. Jolly, who sat cross legged, her gown stretched tight across her lap, pressed back into the side of the nest. She screwed up her pretty face at the mention of worms, but Paunch looked lively-bright from his bare feet to the points of his ears. He rolled up to his knees, leaning forward.

Gennis put a hand on her brotherling's shoulder and spoke quickly before her brotherling could speak, "These berries are more than excellent. Thank you again, Costard."

"We would be dried up nestlings if it was not for your help our hero-friend." Jolly said.

"Or we would be skin scratched nestlings." Paunch added in a jokely tone.

"It would be murder most foul from Feral the flesh-scratcher and his gang of villains. Mine own nest mates grew up in yon wild wood, but the scratchers climbed to the nest when we had just begun to fly, and carried away . . . ."

Horrified, Gennis stopped Costard before he could give Jolly and Paunch dream-worries. "Please, do not, Costard. It is too sad-tragic."

"Thou hast spoken rightly, Gennis, fair one." Costard hurried to reassure the pocket fairies when he added, "This warm-bright place hangeth far above the milling mob of Feral the flesh-scratcher. Like thine own nest in the sky—most well done by thy parentlings."

Finally, with their stomachs full, the mention of Feral's name and Costard's observation about the safety of their sky-nest reminded the nestlings of their quest to find their motherly and fathling.

"Gennis, did you hear the falsely Feral say that he knows where our parentlings are?" Paunch asked.

"Do you think he might really know?" Jolly brightened.

Costard offered, "Perhaps it's the one true thing he did say. Feral uses bits of truth betimes to catch his hapless victims. Feral the flesh-scratcher cometh and goeth most frequently and knoweth the comings and goings of many small and dearly things in Middleburg."

"But how do we make him tell?" Paunch wondered.

"If he is one that knows, then maybe there are more who know. One of that flesh scratching gang who is not so clever-quick and can be caught," Gennis said, thinking out loud.

"Forsooth, the heart fills with the hope of it. Rest anon, and I will search both high and low for thee and for a way to find thy brave parentlings, my young wingless ones." Costard flapped from sight, his wings stirring the air in the nest. The nestlings sat in a swirl of feathers. The breeze blew Gennis and Jolly's hair into their faces. They brushed it out of their eyes.

Jolly, Paunch, and Gennis watched Costard soar away into the wide-big sky, their chins resting comfortably on the edge of the nest.

Jolly said, "I am very tired of watching others fly away."

"Me too," Paunch said.

Gennis back-patted her sisterly and said, "Soon, Jolly, our wings will grow. Soon, I hope. But you flew. Was it fine-bright?"

Jolly laughed, "I did not really fly, but when I closed my eyes I could dream-wish." She closed her eyes and said, "Yes, it was fine-bright."

In a softer voice Jolly said, "I thought that I would never see you again when you and Paunch fell downly."

Gennis reached for her sisterly's hand and said, "I know."

"That was a very darkly-dark feeling, Gennis," Jolly said.

Paunch nodded in agreement.

Gennis thought a moment and said, "Yes, but we are herely now. Perhaps the world is not as wide-big as we thought, since we have found each other again, and Costard, a true friend, and a place to be safe for a time. We are here now and the darkly feeling is smaller.

We are going to find our motherly and fathling, and we are going to be tight-fast together again. Perhaps we are not too bit-small for the wide-big outside."

Gennis used firmly words that made Jolly and Paunch feel better. The nestlings sat back waiting for Costard to return. They trusted in their new friend and in Gennis' firmly words.

Chapter Ten

The Skink Brothers Whooten

Paunch had fallen asleep to the sound of sisterly voices, and when he finally woke up the sun hung fat and lazy in the westerly sky. His hair stuck up in a wild tangle as he rubbed the sleep-sand from his eyes. Costard had not returned. But Jolly and Gennis watched the sky, searching for him. Occasionally the-digging-in-the-dirt pockling with his deep-down pocket full of tools, the very pockling that had carried Gennis and Paunch to Jolly, poked his head out of his darkly hole, and he wondered why he still felt a little tickly. The bulldozing monsterly still chugged and snorted across the street, pushing and shoving at broken trees and rubbish. And the nestlings still felt overly smallish in this wide-big world of pockling work and flesh scratching trickery, despite Gennis' firmly words. From inside Costard's nest their adventures felt almost like part of a dreamly story told at bedtime by Fathling.

Since Gennis and Paunch had climbed up to Costard's nest, Jolly had not been able to stop hugging Gennis for more than a shortly minute. Jolly quit hugging Paunch only when he had curled up to nap. When Jolly wasn't hugging Gennis she was holding Gennis' hand. But it was when Paunch sat up and blinked his sleep-slow eyes in the sun that Jolly squeezed Gennis' hand so hard that it hurt.

Gennis said, "Jolly, stop. I am right here. I am not going. . . ."

"Gennis, shhhhhhhh . . . be quiet. There are dragons," Jolly warned.

"Drag . . . ?" Gennis turned to look.

A pair of five-striped skinks, their lizard skin gleaming like polished jewels, clung with gripping claws to the wall just above Costard's nest.

"Jolly, I do not think that those are drag . . . ."

"Shhhh, those are dragons, small ones to be sure, and even if that one is missing his great dragon's twitchly tail," Paunch said, sounding wide awake now and very sure of himself. At the word dragons, Paunch had come instantly and completely awake. Dragons were one of Paunch's favorite subjects.

Gennis tried not to laugh at her sisterly and brotherling. "Jolly, I really do not think that those are dragons."

Jolly whispered, "They are. I know it. But, I thought they would be bigger. Did you not think so, Paunch? They are very smallish, but they have a dragon's slickery skin and terrible curve-sharp claws." Jolly showed them a dragon's terrible curve-sharp claws with her fingers. The two skinks looked at each other and then at the nestlings. Paunch made curve-sharp claws with his fingers.

The Skink Brothers Whooten did have slickery dragon skin that glittered under the golden sky, and the tips of their noses shimmered black. Five yellow stripes streaked along their sleek skink bodies. Their lips turned up at the corners in shy smiles.

"Do you think they will fire-scorch us with their dreadful dragon breath?" Jolly wondered. The smiling skinks blinked their marble bright eyes at Jolly.

Paunch asked, "Why do they not have great fanning wings?" He was always ready to talk about dragons, their dreadful dragon breath and their great fanning wings.

Jolly shrugged, "I do not know, Paunch."

"Ahhh, of course," he said, "they are fresh-new like us." He sounded pleased at having worked out the problem of smallish, wingless dragons.

Paunch decided to do a bravely thing and yelled, "Be gone, dreadful, dank dragons. Be gone."

Jolly snorted, "You cannot shoo dragons. Dragons need Motherly's magic, or a dragon orb, or a charmly sleep spell. Everyone knows that, Paunch." Even though Jolly snorted at Paunch's efforts, she started helping Paunch by waving her arms too.

The marble eyes blinked again and then the skinks said politely, "We are Frit and Jut, the Skink Brothers Whooten." They spoke in sing-song unison, sounding very polite and un-dragonly.

But this only confused Jolly and Paunch, who expected dragons to be more foul-fierce. Gennis laughed out loud. Paunch started to wave a bare elderberry branch at the puzzled skinks.

"Go away, dragons, away—be gone!" Paunch shouted and waved. Jolly curved her fingers and growled.

"Dragons?" Jut wondered.

"No," Frit assured.

"Skinks," Jut repeated.

"Yes," Frit agreed.

"The Skink Brothers Whooten," they said together. They spoke a little louder this time, thinking that the young fairies were quite possibly hard of hearing. Gennis held her middle as she laughed at the stalemate. Paunch and Jolly insisting on dragons and the skinks insisting on being, well—skinks.

"Leave Costard's nest at once," Jolly ordered.

Hearing the familiar name, Jut Wooten called out, "Costard, yes, yes. Costard is our friend, also. We are here to provide services for friends of our friend, Costard."

Gennis pushed past her waving brotherling and growling sisterly and asked, "What do you mean, services?"

"Costard did not speak of it? Then I will speak of it. We are Jut and Frit Whooten, the Skink Brothers Whooten—Demolition, Salvage and Relocation our specialty," Frit said, not without pride.

"I am Gennis, and these are Paunch and Jolly," Gennis said, introducing her family, and then with a twinkle she added sweetly, "brave-bright dragon hunters." The Skink Brothers Whooten chuckled politely.

Confused, Jolly demanded, "But you must be dragons with your slickery skin."

"Not at all. We have skink skin which we think is nicer than either dragon skin or even lizard skin," said Frit. He twitched his stump of a tail.

"But we once stole a dragon's egg," Jut added helpfully, his tail whipping elegantly side to side. A discreet cough interrupted Jut.

"Not egg stealing, but egg relocating," Frit explained.

"Yes, exactly," Jut quickly agreed.

Paunch, still holding his dragon-fighting elderberry branch, was instantly fascinated and demanded, "A dragon's egg? Where did you take it? How long did you keep it? Did you see it hatch? Did you not have worry-concern, and what about its fiercely-foul motherly?" Gennis finally clamped her hand over Paunch's quickly mouth.

"A story for another time, perhaps?" Gennis warned. The skinks blinked and smiled.

Everyone was startled when Costard's grey wings fanned the air over the nestlings as he settled on the nest's edge. A single pinfeather drifted over the edge of the nest to the ground.

"You are well come, friends?" Costard said. The skinks nodded politely. Paunch hid the elderberry branch behind his back. He and Jolly had the good sense to look down at their toes when they heard Costard call the skinks by the help-name friend.

"'Now we plot trouble most foul' for the villains that may have thine parentlings," Costard quoted and dropped a long, twisting loop of dirty string at the nestling's feet.

The three nestlings put their heads together and leaned in close to hear what Costard and the Skink Brothers Whooten would say about a plot-plan.

Chapter Eleven

Plot-Plan

Jut and Frit Whooten looked exactly the same from their noses right up to their tails. Jut's tail was long and sleek and came to a sharp-clean point, but Frit's tail ended in a nubbly lump of a stump. The Skink Brothers Whooten bobbed their heads in perfect imitation of one another as Costard began to speak.

"The Brothers Skink have agreed to aid thee, and wave their customary fee, in thy fine and noble quest to find thy parentlings, mine young pocket fairies, also mine friends," he said.

Jolly, Gennis, and Paunch smiled at the word friends.

Jut Whooten added eagerly, "Frit's tail is a matter of honor, not payment."

Curious, but too shy to ask about Frit's tail, Jolly and Paunch leaned forward, their eyes moon-round as Gennis asked for all of them, "What happened to your honorable tail?"

"Those flesh-scratching devils tried to make a dinner, snack, feast, meal out of Frit, but Frit was one fast skinkly," Jut said, as he bobbed his head at his brother.

"Not fast enough," Frit offered, waggling his stumply tail.

Paunch said, "Better without a tail than being a quickly snack."

The scaly heads bobbed faster, their marble eyes shining.

Frit said solemnly, "May my tail have left a bad taste in those flesh-scratching mouths."

"May it be so," Jut agreed.

Costard interrupted, "And thus the Skink Brothers Whooten have offered their good aid for thy quest."

Costard pecked at the long loop of twine that he had dropped into the nest at the feet of the nestlings. He said, "We must now plot-plan to catch a scratcher."

"And if those flesh-scratchers do not want to say where to find your motherly and your fathling, we will make them want to," Jut said.

Frit Whooten sounded confident and determined when he added, "Listen to Costard's plot-plan, younglings."

The skinks bobbed, and Gennis, Jolly, and Paunch scooted close to listen.

"Lower . . . and . . . lower, down, now . . . stop," Frit's voice sounded official and firm-solid as he called up to the nestlings.

They tied a loop with Costard's twine after threading the twine in and around the letter *"O"* in the word *Go* in the sign *Gas-N-Go*. It took all three of them because the twine was thickly in the hands of the

three pocket fairies. Costard watched as they prepared for their part of the plot-plan. He tipped his head to see the loop of twine puddled on the ground below.

Paunch clapped and congratulated Costard, "A perfect piece of catch-twine for this catcher's trap." Costard puffed out his feathers, pleased.

The plan was to send Frit Whooten skittering along as bait and to catch a greedy flesh-scratcher in the loop of twine as the scratcher ran after Frit. He was anxious to redeem himself in his own eyes for what he considered the foolish loss of a perfectly useful and shimmery tail.

From the sky, Costard was to give the signal, and the nestlings would set-spring the trap by pulling the loop tight. Hopefully, they would catch one of Feral's gang at the end of a smart-bright plan.

The Whooten Brothers crept along the foundation of the *Gas-N-Go* until they clung temptingly near the corner of the building, twitching one tail and one stump in rhythm. Everyone, the nestlings with their hands fist-tight on the looped twine, Costard dipping and hovering on the warm breezes above, and the skink brothers, their bodies dancing in time, watched for any sign of one of those yowling, skulking flesh-scratchers. The plot-plan was set.

Jut twitched his lovely tail with its elegant stripes knowing how irresistible twitching can be to flesh-scratchers. Without a tail, Frit just pumped his legs up and down and thumped his tail stump to attract attention and to warm up his running muscles for the chase.

Predictably, a raggy, sad flesh-scratcher crept out from behind the *Gas-N-Go* garbage dumpster. She caught sight of the skinks and was fascinated by their pumping, twitching, striped bodies. She watched for a long while, her eyes fixed.

Costard hovered just overhead. When he mimicked a crow's deep *caw-caw* the nestlings knew to be ready with their end of the coiled catch-twine. Paunch held his breath. Jolly made a star-wish and Gennis tightened her grip.

The flesh-scratcher, a scrawny one, could not resist the idea of delicious skink for dinner. So she crouched and crept towards the building, crawling along the hedge at the base of the *Gas-N-Go*, twisting in and out of the branches and trunks. Still, Costard could see her mudly fur through the green, and when the scratcher sprang at the

Skink Brothers Whooten, Costard made the high roaring screech of a falcon.

At the signal Paunch yelled, "Run! Go!"

Frit Whooten flew along the base of the pockling *Gas-N-Go*, skittering over the bricks, across a glass door, and finally to where the nestlings clutched their end of the catch-twine. Jut watched the race. He signaled to Costard.

Costard quoted, "'Pull hard and catch the swaggering rascal!'"

Gennis, Paunch, and Jolly tugged on their end of string. Shocked and excited at the sudden, heavy weight they felt, they looked at each other and yank-pulled harder. Far below, they could hear the spitting, yowling, crying of what could only be a fast-caught flesh-scratcher. Paunch pulled hard and tied the snare tight to a metal bracket holding the *Gas-N-Go* sign to the bricks behind the nest, and then Paunch, Jolly, and Gennis raced to the edge of the nest to see who dangled by one tabby foot beneath them.

※

The tabby flesh-scratcher snarled and hissed, but soft-low. "You don't know Feral. He will hurt me dead. I cannot tell you anything about your motherly or fathling."

"Will dealing with Feral the flesh-scratcher be worse than to be left hanging here for the pocklings to find? Worse than that?" The Skink Brothers Whooten clung to the wall just above the slowly swinging flesh-scratcher.

"Do not leave me for the pocklings. I am a motherly of young, myself. My kittens will die without me. I don't know anything! Pleasssssseeeee?"

"I faith think it unlikely that thou knowest nothing. I have oft seen thee at Feral's right paw." Costard flapped. "And perhaps thou art a motherly, or perhaps thou art not," he added.

It felt wrongly and itchy to the nestlings to listen to this conversation happening so far below them, and Paunch yelled down, "Tell us now, you stinkly, where our parentlings are, or you will deal with Paunch Moon Climb." Paunch leaned over and shook his fist in the air.

Gennis grabbed her brotherling's shoulder, afraid he would topple from yet another high place and wind up hanging upside down, red faced and embarrassed. Gennis cautioned Paunch, "Perhaps she is a motherly to young."

Frit calmly offered, "Your younglings will be fine if you tell us what you know about the pocket fairy parentlings from the sky-nest. We will let you go."

"How do I know that you will let me go if I say where the fairy folk might be?" Tabby Scratcher whined.

Jolly piped up, "Because we are not lie-makers. If we say it, then it is so."

Tabby Scratcher did not think her chances good either way, no matter what she did. But even the thought of having the pocklings catch her was making her mouth very dry and her fur hurt. She was also very dizzy, but she thought that might be because she was very tired of swinging back and forth by one paw. No young scratchers were waiting for her, but no one needed to know that. Better to tell what she knew and go away fast, before Feral grabbed her up. If she stayed here she would be captured by the pocklings for sure, and maybe they would make a stew out of her.

"Tell us what you know," Jut sounded calm and patient, "or I will lure Feral here myself."

This made Tabby Scratcher's tongue move ready-fast. Besides, her ears had begun to ring from being upside down so long.

"Remember you must let me go for my young scratchers," Tabby whined again, "and yes, okay, yes, the two pocket fairies, Nanda and Marker, who live high in the sky-nest, are in a glass trap—inside the pockling den."

The flesh-scratchers called the *Gas-N-Go* a den, not understanding about pockling ways or pockling words. Like most creatures, the scratchers thought their words the only words worth saying.

"Feral and me, we saw the spotty-faced pockling called Ralph put the fairies in the glass trap. Feral said the pocklings call it a pickle jar, that glass trap."

Here was a startling clue, those pockling words. How could Tabby know what pocklings call traps for pocket fairies? The nestlings leaned farther over the edge of the nest and Costard cocked his head to hear.

Tabby hissed, "The spotty-faced one, the one who opens the doors of the den, caught the fathling when he was damaged by the wind. The motherly he trapped after that, when she came to help the fathling."

Frightened by strangely words like glass and jar, Jolly covered her mouth with a hand that shook a little and asked her brotherling and sisterly, "What is a pickle trap-jar?"

"I do not care what it is, but I know it is where Motherly and Fathling are kept-caught," Gennis said.

"I know what pickles are," Paunch offered, "because I love Motherly's rabbit-grass-seed pickles, but I do not know about this glass-pickle-trap-jar."

Below them, the skink brothers chewed at the twine holding the still talking flesh-scratcher, keeping their promise to let Tabby Scratcher go. She not only told them where they could find Nanda and Marker, but also the location of a troll's treasure and a fish carcass left over from her dinner.

"I would like one of Motherly's pickles right now," Paunch said, looking dreamly and wistful, forgetting for a moment the serious sadness of their parentlings' situation.

Gennis sunk back into Costard's nest, balled her fists at her side and said, "We will not let some spotty-faced pockling keep our motherly and fathling in any pickle trap-jar."

"Do not say pickle trap-jar, Gennis," Jolly whispered. "It makes me want to eye-leak."

"Pickles are almost as good as butter bread and bee honey," Paunch said, dreaming out loud. "Do you think pickle jars have a lot of pickles in them?"

"I think that right now there is one of these pickle trap-jars with our parentlings in it, Paunch, and that we should be thinking of a way to get them out of there," Gennis barked at her brotherling.

"Paunch," Jolly muttered between her fingers, her hands over her face, "I don't think you should be talking with your middle-gut right now."

Paunch felt sad-false when he realized what he had been doing and he apologized, "I am sorry Gennis, Jolly. I will do better. I was just dream-wishing that we were all together again talking about dinner and counting rabbit-grass-seed pickles."

Gennis and Jolly, their faces frumped and frowning, scooted close to Paunch and back-patted him, understanding his dream-wish. They also understood that it might be some time before their talk would be about pickles, fishing, or family dinner.

Chapter Twelve

The Spotty-Faced Pockling Called Ralph

O h, Gennis, look up. Our nest is glow-bright again," Jolly's voice, excited now instead of griefly, drowned out the sounds of the spitting flesh-scratcher and the string-chewing skink brothers below Costard's nest. Gennis could see the bright flash of yellow, red, and green in the sky. A blue spill of light from the *Gas-N-Go* sign fell over Jolly's hair and Paunch's frownly face. The glow bathed everything in the nest with its gleam-bright shine. All around the nestlings the world stirred awake with hums, whirs, and flashing as the pockling magic came back after the wild-salt-zebra-wind.

The smiling face of their digging-in-the-dirt pockling popped out of his hole in the ground to watch the traffic lights. Gennis realized that their pockling with his luck-big pockets had been working to make their nest lights glow again. *He is a maker of lights, like me.* Gennis smiled, thinking of her own gifting magic and bright fairy lights that dance in the dark. The traffic light glowed red, green, and then yellow.

A pitiful yowl, followed by spitting and crying, brought the nestling's attention back to the trouble below them. "Let me go. They'll be coming now that the pockling light magic is back. I have answered your questions. I've said where Nanda fairy and Marker fairy are."

But Costard was not finished with the stinkling, Tabby Scratcher. "But how canst the yon pocket fairy nestlings get to their parentlings?" Costard said, flapping. The Skink Brothers Whooten paused in their chewing.

"I can't know that, foolish flyer," the flesh-scratcher choked on panic now.

"You seem to know a great deal about the comings and goings of these pocklings and their captives. Has all been made known?" Costard asked.

"I only saw them taken into the den. Any more I do not know. Perhaps Feral knows?"

Paunch yelled down, "Where should we look inside? How do we get in? What does the spotty-faced pockling want with them?"

Tabby spit back, "I do not know. The spotty-faced pockling kicks us with his foot or chases us with his boom-broom if we come near the entrance of his den. All I can say is what I said. Let me go! I want to run away before the spotty-faced pockling comes, or Feral. I want to run away from you, most of all."

Jut and Frit offered, "Running would be our suggestion. Feral will bite off more than your tail if he catches you, and the spotty-faced one will call the pockling scratch-catchers." They bobbed their heads in agreement.

"It is only our opinion," Frit said.

"Yes, correct, only our opinion," Jut added.

Paunch and Gennis were growing even more twitch-itchy. Gennis called down, "Tell us everything you know."

"I can't," Tabby Scratcher wailed.

Paunch yelled, "When will the spotty-faced pockling come back?"

"Ohhhh, soon, I know it. I know it. The lights have come back on."

They turned as they heard a spluttering chug coming from down Middle Street and Jolly cried, "A rusher-rumble-by is coming!"

The flesh-scratcher yowled but still not loudly. "Is it the scratch-catchers?" she asked.

A clunking, sputtering rusher-rumble-by coughed its way into the parking lot with a burp of exhaust. It parked just to the right of Costard's nest and under the *Gas-N-Go* sign. Everyone inside the nest went still, hoping not to be noticed.

Gennis, Paunch, and Jolly peeked over the edge of the nest to see a tallish pockling, with a head full of red hair and a face full of spots, unfold from the front seat of the clunkly green rusher-rumble-by. Through the hedge, Costard and the Skink Brothers Whooten watched carefully as the spotty-faced pockling lumbered by, whistling and swinging a key on a chain. He walked right by the flesh-scratcher behind the hedge, who was doing her very best to look dead.

The pockling walked so close to the three nestlings that for a moment the light from the *Gas-N-Go* sign turned the tops of his ear blue and made the spots on his face look darkly. On his shirt the nestlings could see a name.

"R-a-l-p-h," Paunch spelled out under his breath. "His name is Ralph, Gennis."

"He is going right by us, the cruel-tight pockling that stole Motherly and Fathling," Jolly whispered.

Gennis warned, "Be quiet Jolly. You too, Paunch."

Paunch spluttered at her, "But Gennis, he is here."

"I know," Gennis said.

Gennis leaned over the edge of the nest as far as she dared and waved to Costard. With his quickly eye Costard saw her wave and flapped up to the nestlings, startling the pockling. Laughing nervously in surprise, the spotty-faced Ralph waved at Costard, trying to frighten him. Costard flapped his wings and settled near his nest where the three pocket fairies crouched.

The pockling walked by muttering, "I need to clean that stupid nest out of that stupid sign, stupid bird."

Gennis crept over to Costard. "Costard, he has them," she said.

"I knowest it well," Costard confirmed.

Paunch whispered fiercely, "He is getting away."

"Costard, can you get me close enough . . . ."

Costard interrupted, "I see thine plan, bold one. Art thou sure?"

"Costard, hurry, before he disappears." Gennis cautioned Jolly and Paunch, "Stay tight-fast in Costard's nest, I am going to find Motherly and Fathling." Jolly jumped to her feet, her hands balled into fists. Paunch's mouth dropped open in shock.

"Hey," Paunch yelled to Gennis as she jumped from the edge of the nest to Costard's back between his wings, "we want to go too."

Jolly cried, "Do not go, Gennis."

"There is not enough room for all of us to fly. Let the flesh-scratcher go, Paunch."

"But Gennis, what are you going to do? How will we find you?" Paunch asked.

"I'm going to find out why this pockling needs to keep pocket fairies in pickle trap-jar and where. Be ready."

"Ready for what?" Jolly cried.

"Ready for adventures to happen!" Gennis yelled over her shoulder at Paunch and Jolly as she gripped Costard's feathery neck. "Be daring!" she cried.

Costard flapped his wings once, and then Gennis was gone. Jolly and Paunch waved goodbye from Costard's nest and then felt silly for waving. Gennis had not looked back.

Costard and Gennis flew close to the spotty-faced pockling named Ralph as he stood in front of the front door of the *Gas-N-Go*.

Startled, Ralph slapped at Costard and yelled, "Your days are numbered, bird."

Gennis bent close to Costard's neck, her hands full of feathers. The rush of wind in her face made her eyes water.

The spotty-faced Ralph had the hump of a canvas pack on his back. He turned and jammed a silver key into the keyhole of the cracked glass door. He kicked a tree branch out of the way so the door would swing freely.

Gennis stayed low between Costard's wings as he flew close to the pockling. Gennis needed to think of her motherly and fathling fast-trapped only once to find the strength to leap from Costard's back onto the pockling's backpack. The door rattled and Gennis Star Milk, daughter of Nanda Star Shimmer and Marker Best Moon, clung to the backpack, waiting to disappear into the dankly den of the spotty-faced pockling called Ralph.

Chapter Thirteen

Gennis the Daring

Gennis clung to Ralph's backpack, feeling determined in her mind and in her heart to find her parentlings. She was going where this spotty-faced pockling went, and she was going to find out what this spotty-faced pockling knew. The backpack thunked and bumped and Gennis grabbed tight-fast, but even the most determined of nestlings can lose her grip.

After the tink-clink of keys against metal rattled in Gennis' ears, the spotty-faced Ralph pushed his way through the door. Gennis could see the sky's reflection dance in the glass-glitter of the door. Ralph walked inside the *Gas-N-Go* with Gennis cling-tight. He shrugged his shoulder, making the backpack shift and wobble, and Gennis lost her tightly grip. Falling like a leaf, Gennis clamped her lips shut.

Suddenly, smooth metal felt cool under her hands and she grabbed—hard. Swinging from a silver ring on the side of the backpack, Gennis clamped her hands tighter around the metal ring, closed her eyes, took a breath, and thanked every brightly sky-star she could think of that she hadn't fallen underneath the pockling's stomping feet. When she finally opened her eyes she couldn't hold back one thin yelp, because she found herself staring into the jeweled eyes of a tiger-striped flesh-scratcher with point-sharp teeth.

Gennis came very close to letting go of the metal ring until she realized that the eyes staring into hers were stone and the teeth painted. This flesh-scratcher was not real. It was just a decoration hanging from the silver ring that Gennis had grabbed when she fell. Gennis stared at the pointly teeth and laughed, wishing Paunch was here to share in the joke.

Gennis dangled next to the tiger face and several jangling silver keys. The door rattled shut, and Gennis was inside the *Gas-N-Go*, a cavernous den of pockling marvels.

Gennis' fingers ached. She tried not to slip again as the spotty-faced pockling turned knobs and pressed buttons, making bells ring and lights blink. She bounced against the backpack as a delicious odor poured over Gennis when Ralph made a pot of water the color of fall leaves tumble-boil.

Finally, everything—backpack, keys, grinning tiger face, and Gennis—tumbled to the ground, and Gennis rolled into a dusty corner. After checking her elbows and knees, Gennis crept slowly and carefully forward so that she could peek around the tumble-down backpack.

The inside of the *Gas-N-Go*, which felt to Gennis like an enormous cave was stuffed with more pockling curiosities than Gennis could have ever guessed at or imagined. Nothing Fathling had told her about the pockling world could have prepared her for this.

Great towers of bright, screaming color reached to the sky—boxes, bags and bundles. Pockling faces smiled at her from everywhere and pockling words marched across every available surface. Colors, shapes, and numbers lined up in rows and rows. Pockling food and drink were all arranged in neat pyramids and towering stacks. Gennis recognized bread shaped into loaves taller than two of her. The air smelled full and rich. She breathed dozens of smells, some sweetly, some sharply.

The world outside had been wide-big, but this den-cave-nest-world was a jolt-shock to her eyes and thinking. It felt like a charmly spell that made Gennis feel confused and lost. She saw so many unknowable things with so many unknowable uses. Gennis wondered how long it would take to understand all the magic in this one place or even to find two smallish pocket fairies in this great pockling den.

She also knew that there was no ease-magic here that she could use to find her parentlings. This magic was too trick-hard for her. She was going to have to be Gennis the smartly if she was going to find her motherly and fathling in all this eye-muddle.

In her corner, Gennis felt so bit-small on the floor that a whimper started to grow in her throat and threatened to close-choke her voice and her courage to death. She shook off the darkly mood because she knew that being little wasn't as big a problem as being without a bravely plan and a true heart. She also knew that pocket fairies without wings did not do very well on the ground where they can be flat-mashed. So Gennis looked up-straight for answers. If she could just be as up-tall as that spotty-faced pockling, Ralph, she might be able to see beyond the tallest stacks where her parentlings might be waiting in a pickle trap-jar.

The answer stretched up in front of her face just to her left. It was a metal climb-up shaped like a ladder. It was full of smooth, shiny, bookly pages. Those pages had more smiling pockling faces and grinning pockling teeth. The bookly pages said things like *Lose Ten Pounds Like Magic* or *Men in the Moon Send Secret Messages with Stardust.* Gennis realized that if she could reach the top of this climb-up she would be at the top of the highest tower in the pockling den. And she concluded that would be as fine a place as any to look for Motherly and Fathling.

Gennis stood at the bottom of the climb-up in her bare feet. One big toe throbbed when she scratched the back of one leg with her foot. She couldn't remember when she had hurt her toe. Her skirt had gotten ripped, but she didn't know when. She felt gritty and dirty. Her hair was a wild tangle down her back. Tipping her head back, Gennis couldn't see the top of the climb-up. It seemed, from where she stood, to be a long-off climb. Gennis didn't know what else to do.

She climbed. The climb was not very hard, but it was up-straight.

When there wasn't anywhere to reach with her hands, Gennis simply shimmied up the sides of the climb-up, her bare feet pressing against the cool metal. Up over the pictures of grinning lips and teeth Gennis climbed, thinking how ticklish it would be to have some small something creep-crawl across your upper lip or eye. When she climbed past a bookly page called *The National News Finder* her foot slipped a little. On the front page was a picture of what was supposed to be the smirkly, smiling face of a bush troll, and the words underneath read *Troll Spotted on City Bus, Reward Offered for Its Capture.* Not only was it not a true-real bush troll, it wasn't even a goodly drawing of a bush troll.

Gennis shrugged and said to herself, "Everyone knows bush trolls never smile." She kept climbing. She thought that pocklings must be easy to fool if they could think that picture was anything close to being a true-real troll. She puzzled about foolish trickery and silly foolishness as she climbed. And she wondered at the kind of pocklings who would want to capture small and dearly things for a reward.

Some of the bookly pages left smears of inkly black on Gennis' hands as she climbed, making her hands slickery. By the time she reached the top of the bookly ladder, Gennis was more anxious than ever for wings because her arms burned and she was a bit out of breath. But being on the countertop made Gennis appreciate how wonderful being above the beneath can be. She could see the whole place—bottom, top and middle. But as hard as she looked, she still could not see any place where Ralph might be hiding a pickle trap-jar full of pocket fairy parentlings.

Gennis peeked from a tight-safe place on the countertop behind a container made of glass. It was full of metal disks. Those disks made her think of treasure with their carved faces of pocklings on one side and fierce looking rise-higher flyers on the opposite side. Through the glass Gennis noticed a sign. She inched around to read it. The sign read, "*Help Change a Child's Life – Donate Now.* PLEASE HELP FILL THIS JAR." She read the pockling words again. A jar! This is a jar! A slickish, glassy, treasure jar!

She looked through the glass of the jar and thought about her parentlings being inside. Gennis turned and searched again for a likely spot for two pocket fairies to be trap-kept. She touched the clear surface behind her, shivered at its chill-cool feel, and wondered how anything, pocket fairy or otherwise, could ever escape from such a slickish place.

She could hear hustling and bustling somewhere in the deep corners of the *Gas-N-Go* from her hiding place, but Gennis could not see what that pockling, Ralph, might be up to. Thinking of being stone-steady and brave-fierce, Gennis climbed even higher. She scrambled to the top of the topmost point on the counter, up and over more numbers and buttons. She read the words *Cash Register* as she scrambled higher and higher. She stretched as up-tall as she could so that she could see.

Gennis could hear Ralph whistling; she strained to understand where the sound might be coming from—maybe some secret place—a room, a cave, or a magic closet. Anything was possible in this strangely place. Gennis was so intent on catching a glimpse of the spotty-faced pockling across the room that when he finally did pop out from behind a door, Gennis gasped, lost her balance, and rolled down the face of the cash register. It wasn't a terrible fall or even a very down-far fall, but it was a fall full of rings, dings, and flashing lights. A cheery bell clanged as a secret drawer popped open. Gennis rolled into it.

Gennis rolled around in a pile of loose, silvery disks—more treasure—so much more. She had seen treasure just like this in the *"Change a Child's Life"* jar, and she wondered how her life would change when Ralph found her crawling around in his trovely-treasure. She gasped when she looked up and saw her inkly handprints all over the treasure drawer. She crept to her knees and listened for the sound of thumply feet coming toward her.

She didn't have long to wait. The sound boomed up and down and grew bigger and bigger. Gennis shook her head to clear it and listened as the pockling thundered towards her and his open treasure drawer.

Chapter Fourteen

Swept Away

Gennis, the daring daughter of Marker and Nanda Sky Weaver Night Shine, had been raised on quick-grass bread, bee pollen soup, and stories of amazing, bravely feats of pocket fairies from the firstly times. If ever Gennis needed to remember to be bravely, it was now. She was rolling around in a pockling treasure trove. Her inkly handprints crawled across the surface of the treasure drawer. And the pockling that the treasure belonged to had heard her fall into his trove. The sound of his feet boomed closer and closer. Gennis thought how wonderful it would be to burrow under that treasure and just disappear.

For a briefly moment, Gennis thought she could hear her parentlings' whispers and feel their breath on her night-bed cheek as they said, "To live afraid is to live smallish. When you get up in the morning, Gennis Star Milk, get up—and live! Always live bright-brave."

Pockling feet tromped closer. Jumping to her feet, Gennis scrambled up, over, and under the open drawer, bending low so that her head would not bump. A great rumble shook the air and ground.

"What is going on with this silly cash register?" Ralph's voice thundered all around her.

The pockling slammed the drawer closed. It dinged into place. He must be able to see Gennis. He had to see her. She was here, *right here*, standing in front of the treasure box, clear-plain, inkly palms sweating.

Sometimes pocklings have a hard time seeing what is right there. They think it should not be there so that means that it cannot be there. This can be lucky for young pocket fairies. So, the drawer got shut and the pockling, Ralph, tromped away. He slipped back behind that open door in the back of the *Gas-N-Go*.

Gennis collapsed against the cash register. But just as the breath started to come back into her chest and the feeling come back into her feet, the sound of stomping grew big again in Gennis' ears. That sound was as big in her ears as the outside sky had felt in her eyes.

The spotty-faced pockling was coming back. Something must be bothering him about his cash register, something that was tickling at the edges of his memory maybe, like inkly handprints. Gennis tried hard to think like a giant, spotty-faced pockling, but the sound of stomping feet made her panic.

At that moment, all Gennis wanted was to become invisible, a much bigger magic than the magic of making fairy lights from light shine. The only magic that Gennis could make now was the magic of doing. Dropping to her knees, she peeked over the edge of the drawer to the dizzy-down ground below.

Then came the sound of a crash, and Gennis heard the pockling mutter rough-red words. She peeked to see that a pile of yellow boxes had tumbled to the ground just in front of Ralph's path. Without waiting to find out how long the mess-fuss would slow him down, Gennis scooted to the center of the treasure drawer and hauled a long length of rope dangling from the key that was still stuck in the keyhole of the drawer. Gennis felt sweat on her lip and between her shoulder blades, but she shrugged it away as she hauled up the loop of rope.

The pockling stopped his red words and marched closer. Gennis pulled harder. She pulled faster. Finally the length of rope lay coiled at her feet just under the drawer. Gennis waited no longer. She grabbed the looped end and jumped.

Just as the spotty-faced Ralph came around the corner, Gennis swung down and across the front of the counter, just underneath the treasure drawer. In a long flowing curve, Gennis sailed through the sky. Like a glider she flew down and up, and then at the height of the curve she sailed back the other way, back and forth, holding on with tight-fast hands. Gennis flew in smaller and smaller swings until she stopped and hung—perfectly still—dangling.

Eyes closed, Gennis let out a tiny, hopeful sigh, wish-wanting that the pockling would still be eye-blind to her. But this time, when she opened her eyes, she stared into one huge Ralphly eye the size of a milk moon in Octoberly.

He said, "Hello there, number three."

Shock-wild, Gennis screamed, let go of her rope, and dropped. The way down had been much faster than the way up, and she landed in a pile of rustling plastic bags that billowed up all around her. Gennis lay still for a moment giving her head a shake, but then she jumped up like a quickly mouse as an enormous hand rushed through the sky toward her, plunging her into shadow.

Gennis darted as Ralph pushed and shoved boxes and sacks. Gennis kept moving, searching for any hole, any safe-sure place, to stuff herself. Scrap paper and dust tumbles rolled wildly as the pockling came after Gennis with a huge broom-sweep. The broom-sweep stabbed at Gennis. Gennis dodged and darted.

Ralph boomed out, "Come here little one. Come to Ralph."

Then he laughed as he sent the broom-sweep whooshing by. Gennis tumbled under the counter.

The broom-sweep stabbed again, and Gennis had no where left to run when a voice, neither big nor small, called to her, "Over here, quick-fast."

Gennis ran toward the darkest corner under the farthest counter, the broom-sweep rushing back and forth behind her. Just as the pockling broom-sweep swept all the boxes and bags away in a great swooshly rush of wind, Gennis dove toward the voice and rolled into the darkness.

Chapⲧer Ɉiɟⲧeen

In the Storm's Eye

Since the wild-salt-zebra-wind, Gennis had dangled from a spider's thread and had been shaken on a wire by a sneak-snake of a Feral flesh-scratcher. She had fallen into a pockling pocket and been carried a pockling mile, and now she had come very close to being swept up by a sweeply broom. Being tight-fast felt sweet to her. But now she was alone in the dark with a wisperly voice, and she was pretty sure that she didn't want to be alone in the dark with only a wisperly voice for company.

Without thinking too much or too long, or worrying that it might not work, or that she hadn't practiced enough, Gennis slapped her hands together and pulled her fingers away from each other, slow-steady; a ball of cheerful fairy light glowed in the palm of her left hand. She took a deep breath and looked into the dark.

The golden circle of fairy light flooded the mousely hole where Gennis stood. From across that circle of light a dazzling smile flashed back at her from an acorn brown face. A tight-snug feeling came over Gennis when she looked at that smiling face. This was no mouse with snickery clicking teeth to bite her. This was no wild troll full of mischief and hurtful words. This was one of the fairy clan, and she knew immediately that he was goodly and kind.

"Did you also fly to this place inside the wild, wet wind?" he asked.

"In . . . inside? Inside the wind?" Gennis sat down hard, stunned and still a little out of breath, the sweeply broom rushing back and forth just outside. Zoa, the pocket fairy, smiled at Gennis' shock. He crossed his sturdy arms across some kind of animal pelt on his chest, laughing. The rest of him was sturdy as well. Gennis could see his strong, bare legs below a kilt decorated with wonderful animal shapes.

The cheerful voice continued, "Inside the wild, wet wind from across the widely salt water where the merfolk swim."

"How can that be?"

"Oh yes, it can be. It was, and it is," he smiled, bowed, and said, "I am Zoa Help Spirit of the straight-tall sky grass where the black-white stripelys dance and the roar-fierce toothlys growl to see it."

"But, inside the wind . . . ?" Gennis remembered how hard their nest had rattled and shook in the hammering zebra wind.

"I flew across the water with my friends, the rise-higher flyers. I had come to the edge of the land to look with my own eyes at the widely salt water, to dance on the golden sand, and to watch the sink-down westernly sun. Then the wind began to twist. At first it was just a small stir of wind in the sand. But then the wind blew too hard to fly against, or even stand against; it was the twistly wind that snatched me up like, well, just like the sand. So, I stayed. And then I saw that other flyers were there, inside the wind with me," his smile never faltered as he spoke.

"In the very middle of the big wind twist, the air is slow-still. I was there. For nine-ish days, we flew inside the wind."

"The wind caught you?" Gennis said, astounded.

The flashing grin grew a little humble and Zoa said, "Yes, and the sink-down sun. I stayed to watch the sink-down sun when the sand began to twist-spin around me. The sand is gold and the water flashes emeralds when the sun falls away. It made me very eye-glad to see it. But it is also the place where baby winds are born, and when they become up-grown they travel all the way to this herely place." Zoa's brown hands danced through the air as he described the sand, wind, and sky.

For the first time Gennis noticed Zoa Help Spirit's beautiful, black-white stripely wings.

"To fly all that long way," she said shaking her head, "so much farther than any pockling mile."

"Some of the time my wings flew, and some of the time I rode on the backs of my rise-higher flyer friends."

Gennis tried to imagine a calm place inside the wild-salt-zebra-wind, but it was hard.

"I can tell you this, that the jeweled merfolk water is broadly and wide, and I was glad for my flyer friends. They are beautiful and brave, those flyers, and smartly about the big sky and wind. They know that inside the storm, there is a great still eye. When you look up you can see the stars hanging quiet above. And inside it is darkly like a harvest night."

"Truly a fine adventure," Gennis sighed.

Zoa sighed deeply, remembering, "A fine adventure."

Gennis asked, "But are you not sadly to be so far from your home? What will you do now?"

Zoa frowned and then smiled as he thought a moment, "Why, I will help you. I am Zoa Help Spirit, and have I not already helped a little?"

Gennis realized that Zoa's introduction called for good manners. She responded solemnly, "Yes, you have helped me more than I can say with word-talk, and I am Gennis Star Milk of the Sky Weaver Night Shine fairy clan, and I am happy that the wild-salt-zebra-wind blew you herely." Gennis stood straight and tall when she spoke, because she was proud of her fine-bright family and saying her kin-names this way made her feel close to her motherly and fathling.

"And I am Zoa, and there is always something to be fixed, or said, or done, or helped."

"I think that is becoming very true for me."

"Why did you need saving from that biggerfolk?"

"Biggerfolk?"

"Yes. Biggerfolk, because you and I are smallerfolk."

"And we call biggerfolks pocklings. I am here because my motherly and fathling are caught-fast somewhere in this pockli . . . biggerfolk place."

Zoa's brown forehead wrinkled in thought, "And that is why I am called Zoa Help Spirit.   I have seen some fairy folk in this pockling place, perhaps. Or I have seen where they are caught-fast, perhaps."

The light in Gennis' hand blazed. Reflected light glittered in Zoa's brown eyes when he looked at Gennis.

He said, "Come and explore a mystery with me."

Zoa grabbed Gennis' hand, the fairy light glowing between their fingers as he pulled her deeper into the mousely hole.

Chapter Sixteen

Through Darkly Tunnels

After Zoa grabbed Gennis' hand and pulled her into the darkly tunnel, they ran. They ran through passages inside the floors and walls made by mice, rattled past nests left by pigmy elves, and zoomed by tunneled openings left by the pocklings themselves. It smelled of mice and mildew. Dust made Gennis sneeze, but Zoa did not slow down even when she sneezed six-ish times.

Zoa zigged quickly this way, and then he sprinted faster that way, up and down beneath the floor and inside the dark places of the *Gas-N-Go* dankly den. Once they passed a motherly mouse and her eight babies in a nest made of bubble wrap who squeaked in surprise as they scrambled by. Zoa stopped only once to check his thinking at an opening with three tunnels. Wires dipped down from the ceiling and twisted along pipes. Water dripped along one wall.

"Where are we going?" Gennis panted.

"To see if I am a good guesser or a great one," Zoa said over his shoulder, but he was moving again, and Gennis followed.

At last, he slowed and then stopped to bend down and peak through the slats of a metal grate. Gennis' fairy light still glowed weakly, but she didn't need it anymore, because light filtered through to them from another room beyond this ease-secret place inside the walls of the *Gas-N-Go.*

"Look carefully, Gennis Star Milk," Zoa said, pointing.

"What will I see?"

"Up there, in that uply place against the wall, like a ledge. There is a brown box. That is a very interesting brown box, I am remembering, because I have seen it move by itself and once almost fall from that uply place. Two-ish times I have seen it move."

As Zoa described what he had seen, Gennis noticed a corner of the box hanging just over the edge of the shelf. The room was full of shelves and boxes neatly stacked, but not that box. It did not sit neatly on its perch.

As Zoa and Gennis watched to see if the box would shake by itself again, the door to the storage room creaked open, and in marched the spotty-faced pockling Ralph. Gennis fell back in surprise, on her bottom-round, even though she knew that he could not see them. Zoa glanced back at her—laugh-happy. Ralph began to count boxes.

"Gennis, you will miss many interesting things while being shake-afraid of that foolish biggerfolk . . . I mean, pockling."

Zoa pressed his face to a slit in the metal, a stripe of light making his eyes gleam.

"Come and watch with me, Gennis Star Milk."

Just as Gennis joined Zoa Help Spirit, the spotty-faced Ralph stopped his counting of boxes and did a strangely thing. Walking to the door, he peeked out, and then he peeked around, and then he closed the door. Next, that pockling put down his counting board, and dragged a chair under that very highest shelf, the very shelf Zoa had just pointed at. Ralph reached for the box, the same box that they had been watching, and he pulled it down. He made a clucking sound deep in his throat as he peered inside, and then he lifted something out of that very interesting move-by-itself box.

It was a jar just like the one with treasure in it, the jar that had said *Help Change a Child's Life*. Only this jar had pocket fairies in it and a silvery lid with holes poked through.

Gennis' fathling, one wing bandaged, sat on a match box frowning at the spotty-faced Ralph. Nanda stood just in front of her husband with her hands on her hips and her eyes glare-bright. Ralph held the jar up high and laughed. Nanda and Marker braced themselves as the spotty-faced pockling turned the jar around so that he could stare at his prize catch from all sides. He laughed again.

Gennis could feel her eyes fill with eye-leak. They were here, lost but now found, angry but alive. They were so close, she felt that they must be able to hear the heart-thump in her chest. It felt as if she had been holding her breath since her motherly had left them alone in the sky-nest, and now she could breathe again—at last.

"I think, Gennis Star Milk, that I am Zoa Help Spirit from the land of the dancing black-white stripelys, and that is your motherly and fathling."

"Yes, Zoa, that is Nanda Star Shimmer of the Sky Weaver Night Shine clan and Marker Best Moon of the Sky Weaver Night Shine clan, my motherly and fathling."

Ralph unscrewed the lid of the jar and put it on a shelf near him. Then he put his fingers into the jar and wiggled them at Nanda. Gennis' motherly ducked away from those great stabbing fingers and Marker shouted something from his seat inside the jar, wincing a little from pain.

"And I must set-free them," Gennis said.

"And I will help you," Zoa said.

Chapter Seventeen

Hot-Bright Flashing Magic

The spotty-faced pockling Ralph stared into the pickle trap-jar and laughed at Marker's anger. Gennis shivered at the grim-dark sound of that laughing. Holding the jar in his hands, he stepped down from the chair. He walked to a stack of boxes marked with the words *Less Wet Paper Towels* and placed the jar on top of it. From his pocket he pulled a smallish box of orange. It was not a wand or a charm sack or a weapon as far as Gennis and Zoa could tell, but there was magic in it all the same; they felt sure of it. The box was the size of his hand, and Ralph waved it at Gennis' parentlings.

"What pockling magic is that?" Gennis whispered as eye-leak threatened to blind her. She pressed her hands against the metal grate in front of her.

"I do not know. This is not a magic that I have seen before." Zoa felt curious and bewildered by the strangeness of this new mystery.

As Ralph had climbed down from his chair, Nanda and Marker had clutched at each other balancing against the movement of the jar. Now Nanda and Marker were clinging to each other, waiting for this latest trouble. Marker gritted his teeth against the pain in his wing.

Addressing Nanda and Marker, the spotty-faced Ralph pointed his curious orange box at them and said, "Now hold very, very still and say cheese."

He pressed the box to his eye and said, "I almost caught another one of you things— brownies, pixies, twixies, or whatever you are, for the family protrait, but it got away."

Gennis felt shakely when she heard this curious charm-spell. Was he trying to turn them into cheese and feed them to some snickery mice?

Ralph pushed a button and an explosion of light filled the room. Flash! He flashed the light box at them, again and again, and each flash made Nanda and Marker blink in the blazing light.

Gennis was afraid for them. She could hear the pockling, between the hot bright flashes, laughing and muttering—some dark-false spell, perhaps. Gennis shuddered again.

Zoa struggled to understand the words and wondered out loud, "What can he mean? 'I'm going to be rich when the tabloids get a look at the two of you?' What kind of creature is this tabloid?"

In her mind, Gennis saw a badly drawn picture of a troll's falsely grin on a bookly page.

Zoa worried, "This sounds like a greed spell. I have no liking for this pockling."

Gennis agreed with Zoa and made a want-wish to be able to yell loud enough to knock that foolish Ralph to the ground, or maybe she could think of some chantly spell of her own to make him smallish, smallish enough to fit inside a pickle trap-jar with holes punched in the top. But she didn't have enough magic yet.

Finally, when Gennis saw her fathling throw his hands up to shield his face against that sharp stabbing light she cried, "I cannot sit-stay and watch this anymore." And without counting, wondering or thinking, Gennis straightened up beside Zoa and squeezed her way through the opening in front of them.

Zoa reached out to catch her hand, "No, Gennis, think. We should think."

"No more thinking. I cannot wait to think," Gennis cried out, as she kept pushing her way into the room where her parentlings remained fast-trapped.

She would not think or wait any more. It was as if all her thoughts and thinking had been used up, and all that she had left was Oberlin fairy clan daring.

Gennis pushed her way onto a mountain of boxes behind the still laughing, light flashing pockling. She could feel Zoa Help Spirit close behind her. The rush of his wings was soft-low.

"Remember, my wings are strong and I can fly. And Gennis, remember you are brave-bright."

He laughed a wild-free-zebra-wind kind of laugh. That laugh spun its way into Gennis' ears as she made another bravely decision.

"I jumped twicely, and I will jump again," Gennis said, referring to her ride into this dankly den, and before she could wonder, worry, wish for wings or more courage, Gennis jumped in a grand leap.

She was barely able to grab a fist full of pockling shirt before the bump on his shoulder and the sound of buzzing in his ears sent the spotty-faced Ralph twirling about to see what had come for him. Swatting at the noise, he swung around trying to smack at Gennis and swat at Zoa.

The three, Gennis, Zoa, and Ralph, started to whirl about in a crazy dance. Gennis pinched him hard through his red name-shirt, and Zoa buzzed close to his ears and eyes. In the storage closet, Ralph's mad weaving and twisting sent boxes crashing into each other. Once Ralph twirled about so madly that he crashed dizzy-down to the ground. One stack of boxes tipped into another, then another stack tipped, and then the pickle trap-jar began to rock.

The Ralph swatted and shouted, "Get away from me!"

Gennis shouted back, "Let my parentlings go!"

Zoa exulted, "Free the fairy folk!"

Thinking that he must be under attack by a whole fleet, flock, or herd of crazed and vicious creatures that pinched and bit and probably had poisoned stingers, and seeing his prize in danger of falling, the spotty-faced Ralph grabbed his precious jar, sending Nanda and Marker

sprawling. Ralph clutched the jar close to his chest looking for somewhere to run and hide.

This pockling should think better of his greed spell when it came to Gennis' parentlings, Zoa thought, as he pulled a nose hair right out of one gaping nose hole. Ralph hollered. Zoa plucked an eyelash.

Holding the jar under one arm, he spun around in tipsy circle. A pinching, biting Gennis clawed at his back and a poking, buzzing Zoa scratched at one great pockling eye, and that sent the spotty-faced pockling staggering backwards through the door of the *Gas-N-Go*. The door smashed open. And with a thud, Ralph, Gennis, and Zoa crashed into the alley.

Chapter Eighteen

Jolly's Gifting Magic

I t was a blue, plastic trashcan that saved Gennis Star Milk from being flat-mashed. That light-flashing, pocket-fairy-snatching, spotty-faced pockling called Ralph fell through the back door of the *Gas-N-Go*, tripped over the garbage cans and rolled around on the ground trying to get away from the small but painful presence of Gennis Star Milk and Zoa Help Spirit. Gennis thanked her star-luck when Ralph didn't fall on top of her and instead landed on one of the tipped over trashcans, breaking his fall and knocking Gennis to the ground. Zoa did everything he could, pulling eyelashes and plucking nose hairs, to keep the foolish pockling on the ground—where he belonged.

Ralph swatted at Zoa and cried like a childling, "Stay . . . away . . . from my nose! You, you are nasty creatures. That hurts. Stop! Stop! You're hurting me!"

When the pockling smacked the front of his face, Zoa flew to the back of his head and pulled the hair on his neck. When the pockling smacked the back of his head, Zoa flew to the front of his face and plucked eyelashes.

In the flurry of falling, rolling, and yelling, Ralph let go of the pickle trap-jar. It rolled out of his hands and clunked against the pavement without breaking. Zoa Help Spirit plucked and pulled. Ralph kept swatting with both his hands, and the jar full of tumbling pocket fairies rolled away.

Gennis crawled on her hands and knees away from Ralph, trusting Zoa to keep him eye-blind and busy. Gennis didn't care so much about tormenting her parentlings' tormenter. She did care about that jar and getting her family, herself, and her new friend Zoa away from here and back to their tight-fast nest where they belonged. She watched as the rolling jar rocked to a stop. It came to rest next to the green dumpster with a tinkling tap.

Gennis yelled to Zoa, "Can you keep him worry-busy?"

Zoa nodded, laughed, tugged at an eyelash and said, "Go."

The pockling yelled, "I'm blinded!"

Gennis brushed herself off and raced toward the pickle trap-jar. She could see her parentlings tumbled about inside the jar, her motherly on her hands and knees and her fathling face down. Incredibly, her fathling was laughing.

"Just like Paunch," Gennis said, and then wondered what Jolly and Paunch were doing, and when they would show up, and how they would know where to find her.

As soon as she reached the jar, she pressed her face to the glass and smiled. Her motherly's eyes were a little wet, but her mouth grin-smiled at Gennis.

Gennis yelled, "We will get you out."

Her motherly's eyes turned grim-tight, and she began to point and wave. Her fathling's face turned even more grim-tight, and he began to point. Gennis knew. Gennis didn't have to turn around. She knew that Feral the flesh-scratcher had found them. And that he was close.

When she did turn, Gennis wanted to cry, because not only was Feral coming for them, but most of his flesh-scratching gang was with him, including Tabby Scratcher, who hobbled along on three paws. Gennis pressed back against the jar, the glass smooth and slick under her hands. Her heart shrank into a hard-tight lump.

"So, here is the brave, little daughter of Nanda and Marker. Did I not say that I would help you and your brotherling find the motherly and fathling?"

Gennis turned her head as Feral's dankly breath filled her face. One of his whiskers brushed her cheek, and when Gennis swiped at it, Feral laughed.

"What did you call me—a maybe false friend? Why, not even close, little one. I like you very much. I have always been a friend to pocket fairies and other smallish things and liked them very much also, and when we figure out how to smash that jar we will like your parentlings very much as well."

"What about the spotty-faced pockling that will hit you with his broom-sweep until you see sparklings?" Gennis said.

"Why, it seems that your pocket fairy mischief has been too much for that poor mistreated pockling of yours, for there he goes."

And there Ralph certainly went, straight through the back door of the *Gas-N-Go*, holding a hand to a newly bald spot on the back of his head and wailing, "What are you nasty things? You've balded me!" The door slammed with a crash as Feral's flesh-scratching gang crept closer.

As he turned and saw Feral, Zoa Help Spirit, having chased off one stinkly threat, figured that he was ready to help Gennis with another stinkly threat, and he flew to stand next to Gennis in front of the pickle trap-jar. His hands rested on his hips, and his black-white stripely wings shimmered in the sky-shine. Inside the jar, Gennis' parents were tight-hugged. Nanda's eyes were tight-closed.

"Gennis, do you have a sharp-smart idea?" Zoa asked without taking his eyes off of Feral. "I am afraid that my gifting magic is to be able to whisper in the ears of stone-strong trunkleys and long-tall necklys and make them laugh. I do not think that that will help me fight this flesh-scratcher."

Feral grinned with sharply teeth.

Gennis thought for a moment and clenched her fist around a hot-bright ball of light shine. When Feral leaned closer, Gennis threw the fairy light as hard as she could. Feral frowned and blinked as the ball of light flew apart and dissolved into white hot sparkles that drifted away on the afternoon breeze.

"Do you think to scare me with fairy lights, foolish little one? No lights and no sharp-smart fairy tricks will save you, and I do not think that Nanda and Marker have any magic strong enough to smash that glass, or they would have done it."

Feral looked at Zoa and said, "Skitter away and we will spare your life, for now. Pulling my tail will not scare me away." Feral loomed over Gennis as he showed his teeth to Zoa. She turned her head and closed her eyes.

"Zoa does not skitter anywhere, you stinkling," Zoa said moving closer to Gennis. "And I think because you are not a truth teller, you may not know how this ending will be. I will stay."

Gennis whispered, "That is not a wisely idea, but I thank you for your heart-help."

Zoa grabbed Gennis' hand and whispered back, "This grand story will be more than fairy dust I think, Gennis Star Milk."

Just then Tabby's familiar voice said, "Why do they always think to fight? Hmmm, Feral?" Tabby Scratcher inched closer.

Another, still more familiar voice shouted from the sky.

"Gennis, look at what I can do."

Shock filled Feral's face as he and the two fairies looked up.

Costard swooped from the sky like a proud eagle, his voice commanding, "Prepare to meet your end, ye bain fools and reckless blackguards."

Jolly and Paunch sat between the bird's wings. Paunch sat in front of Jolly with his arms wrapped around Costard's neck and his mouth full of mockingbird feathers. Jolly sat behind Paunch, her eyes flashing gold and her hair sailing like a white banner behind her. Paunch hooted loudly as Costard dived, but it was Jolly that became the great doer of deeds that day. As Costard dipped, Jolly opened her arms and threw out a black cloud full of boiling white lightening and thrashing black rain.

The cloud, one of those contentious cumulus sorts, floated directly over Feral and his gang and began a fearsome racket—dumping splashing rain and sending bolts of white hot lightening into the milling flesh-scratchers. One bolt struck so near Feral's tail that Gennis and Zoa could smell singed fur.

Paunch yelled, "Hooray, for Jolly. She *can* call clouds but only the black rain clouds, not the happy white ones, which is why it never worked before. How are you Fathling? We've missed you. But Jolly and I have been flying with Costard, and Gennis and I were kidnapped by a pockling pocket after almost getting skin-scratched, and then Gennis jumped on a spotty-faced pockling and left us, and I think that was not very true-fair."

Distracted by the sight of his parentlings and excited to tell them about the adventures they had had, Paunch lost his grip and slipped beneath Costard's neck.

In the meantime, Jolly's storm shook the ground with lightening and drenching rain, blinding everyone and soaking Zoa, Gennis, the flesh-scratchers, and the jar full of pocket fairies.

Gennis and Zoa took their opportunity as soon as the befuddled Feral started to stumble about in the choking downpour, and they slipped behind the jar. When Costard started his second screeching attack this time, pecking at Feral's head, Feral fought back. He sat on his haunches trying to swat Costard from the sky. Jolly threw another angry cloud from her arms. This cloud dumped sharply hail on the needle-toothed scratchers. Zoa and Gennis cheered. Costard dived and pecked. Paunch dangled. Feral yowled and slashed. Paunch kicked. Costard screeched.

Finally Jolly pulled together an oddish, funnel shaped cloud from the air and sent it spinning away in a twistly swirl of wind, rain, and lightening. The twisting cloud swept down over Feral and his now cringing gang. It swept across the pavement, sucking dirt and trash from the ground.

"We are going," one of Feral's followers groaned out as hail thumped down. The funnel cloud twisted faster.

Feral, blinded by rain and hammered by hail, turned to order his followers to stay and fight, only to be sucked up into the hissing, spitting twist of a cloud—a cloud that carried him across the parking lot, through an empty field, over some trees—and away.

In a moment, Feral, his gang, and the roaring clouds were gone. The silence sounded loud in Gennis' ears. Nanda, Marker, Gennis, and Zoa were alone on the ground. Costard glided to a landing. Jolly waved. Paunch finally lost his grip completely so that he dropped with a splash into one of the puddles left by Jolly's storm clouds. Gennis ran to tight-hug her drip-wet brotherling and smiling sisterly.

"Well, I became upside down again, Gennis," Paunch admitted.

"And just at the bestly of times, both of you," Gennis said as she tight-hugged them even harder.

Jolly squeaked between two hiccups, "Oh, Gennis, Motherly and Fathling are still in that pickle trap-jar. I cannot bear it." She hiccupped louder.

Gennis laughed and reassured her sisterly, "Not for long, Jolly. I see two friends that might know what to do."

Gennis pointed to the back wall of the *Gas-N-Go* just above the tipped over blue trashcan where Frit and Jut, the Skink Brothers Whooten, clung tightly to the bricks, bobbing their heads and grinning skinkly grins.

Chapter Nineteen

Strangely Help from a Strangely Place

"We could crack open the glass like an egg," Paunch said, smushing his nose against the jar, making his motherly and fathling laugh.

"While this method may open the jar, it might also damage the fairy parentlings. This would not be a desirable result," Frit said.

Jut Whooten measured the length of the pickle jar with his skinkly feet. Water beads from Jolly's storm magic dripped from the jar onto Frit Whooten's unblinking eyes as he watched Jut.

Fascinated by the engineering and technical challenge the pickle trap-jar presented, the Skink Brothers Whooten settled in to study the freeing of Nanda and Marker. Paunch, who was full of suggestions, suggested rolling the jar, with Motherly and Fathling still inside, back to their sky nest immediately, if not sooner, in case Feral or the other flesh-scratchers should come back. When the obvious problem of how to get the jar off the ground and into the nest was pointed out to Paunch by Gennis, he sadly settled himself in to wait out the problem-solving session, occasionally offering more unworkable ideas.

Gennis pat-hugged her brotherling and asked him how he, Jolly, and Costard had figured out what was happening in the alley behind the *Gas-N-Go*. After all, they had saved Gennis, Zoa, Motherly, and Fathling with perfect, true-bright, pocket fairy timing.

"Well, Gennis, after you jumped on that spotty-faced pockling, and I will tell you that I was feeling madly that you did not invite Jolly and me to go with you—"

Jolly was happy to interrupt. "So he was a big poutling, Gennis, full of skulkings and sighings."

Gennis smiled at their back-and-forthly talk.

Paunch ignored Jolly and continued, "Jolly and I, we decided . . . ."

Jolly was only half-part listening to Paunch; she was still distracted and fascinated with the way the jar made the skink brothers' eyes grow wide-high when they circled the glass. Sometimes their eyes were tiny and black-bright and sometimes the glass made their eyes loom as big as melons. While Jolly watched the skink brothers, she sat very close to the jar with one hand on the glass while her mother pressed her hand to Jolly's through the glass—touching, but not. Gennis kept her hand on Jolly's shoulder while Paunch talked.

" . . . then, Gennis, I remembered to think that sooner or later you would wish-want our help, and that I'd better find out as much as I could so that we could be right where we needed to be, right when we needed to be there."

"And you were. If you had not remembered to be a smart-sharp pocket fairy, well then . . ." Gennis said, letting the sentence trail away.

Zoa, standing quietly next to Gennis, turned to Paunch and said, "I am Zoa Help Spirit from the far land of long-tall necklys and straight-tall sky grass, and I thank you for your perfect knowing and for your perfect arriving."

Paunch stood a little more straightly and clasped Zoa's brown hand. Paunch said, "It was the dust motes. When they were able to settle down after the wild-salt-zebra-wind they had a lot to tell. Some of the dust motes have traveled all the way across the merfolk ocean, but others told me what that spotty-faced pockling plotted."

"I am glad for your gifting magic, Paunch," Gennis smiled at her brotherly.

The Skink Brothers Whooten crawled up the side of the jar and sat on top. "Gennis, is it true that your gifting magic is the making of fairy lights? And do either of your parentlings have the fairy light magic also?" Costard hopped up next to the Brothers Skink, making the jar rock.

Costard addressed the assembly, "Didst not Jolly tell us this truth when she uncovered the mystery of her own gifting magic, that your magic is the making of lights from sky and air? Perhaps your fairy lights and the gifting magic of your parentlings—both together . . . ."

"Motherly can dance water, and Fathling can leaf sail. I don't think that will help," Gennis said.

Jolly put her lips near the jar. "Motherly, Fathling, what should we do to get you out?" Nanda shook her head, and gestured that she couldn't hear Jolly very well through the thickly glass. Marker looked droopy around his shoulders.

"Maybe we could have a dragon melt off the end with his hotly fierce breath. Of course, it would have to be a baby, because a bigly dragon would melt the jar and Motherly and Fathling and the *Gas-N-Go* and me and . . . ." Paunch tried to imagine all the things a dragon's fire would melt.

Just as Paunch's list started to include Zoa's long-tall necklys, a rattling thump followed by a snuffling snuff came from deep inside the green garbage dumpster next to them. Nanda and Marker's pickle trap-jar rocked again, this time from the vibrations inside the big, metal dumpster. Jolly's eyes grew round-wide and Jut and Frit lifted their heads as the sounds bounced and boomed. There was a snork, snuff, and a thump. And those were followed by a snarkly snort. Paunch looked up and noticed one hairy hand curled tight around the rim above them.

Zoa and Gennis jumped back and Costard flew up with a squack as another hairy hand appeared, followed by the craggy face of a bridge troll. On his head, a squashed box with the words, *Three Chocolatier Bars,* dipped over one squinkly eye. His mashed-in nose twitched once and then twice. With a blasting huff, the troll pulled himself over the edge of the dumpster and thumped down next to Zoa. His boxly hat fell to the ground.

No one moved. Jolly started to hiccup again, because it was a fact known that bridge trolls are not only rude, but much, much worse; they are moody. But this troll made his way in the newly world not by living under bridges and rudely demanding tolls from weary travelers; this troll lived wedged tightly inside the green *Gas-N-Go* garbage dumpster, and his most pressing problems were not pocket fairies and their friends, but the yowling flesh-scratchers that tried to steal the tastiest pockling leftovers. And of course, the pocklings themselves who came once a week trying to shake him out of his lovely, cuddly dumpster with an enormous, horned, trash eating, monsterly garbage truck.

The troll, a medium sized one, which is to say that he fit neatly beneath a footbridge but was too large to stuff himself into the blue trashcan, scuffled by. He picked up this bit of trash and that bit of garbage, sniffing and sometimes licking at a grease spot. Once he paused to examine a crate of yellowed newspapers with curled edges; the paper on top of the pile claimed that a baby dragon had been found in a land called Florida near a place called Lake Harney. The troll licked the picture of the baby dragon.

Property of
Middleburg Dumpster, Inc.

Finally, he reached for the pickle jar, his huge hand blotting out Nanda and Marker inside. Zoa had to jump in front of Gennis to hold her back, and Jolly clamped her hand over Paunch's mouth as the bridge troll scratched his rumpled bottom with one hand and jiggled the jar with the other.

"Be still. Wait and see," Costard cautioned from his perch above them.

A bit-quick minute later, the jar lid, squeaking a little, began to turn under the troll's hairy hand.

"Wait and see," Zoa whispered. Gennis took a tightly breath and forced herself to be still and wait.

When the lid toppled off, the troll stuck his entire bumply, smushed nose into the jar and took a sniff. Nanda and Marker's hair stood straight on end, but they didn't seem worry-concerned. Not smelling anything but pocket fairies, the bridge troll tossed the jar away. It landed in the pile of old newspapers, on its side and open. The troll continued snuffling and sniffing. His search was finally rewarded when he found a ring of sweetly bread with a hole in the center and a bite out of one side, and a forgotten bag of deep fat fried chicken gizzards.

Clutching his treasures, the troll jumped straight up, caught the top of the dumpster with one hand, the sweetly bread ring clutched in the other and the bag of gizzards hanging from his mouth, and swung himself back into the comfortable smells and rubbish of his dumpster home. Nothing else came from the dumpster except a burp, followed by a snore, and then silence.

Everyone ran, flapped, or crept to watch Nanda and Marker walk out of their pickle trap-jar prison. Rushing to the opened jar, Paunch, Gennis, and Jolly, followed by their brave-smart friends, helped Nanda and Marker into the brightly day. Nanda and Marker rushed into the hugly arms of their three nestlings—Gennis the Daring, Paunch the Steadfast, and Jolly the Maker of Fierce Rain on Cloudless Days.

Paunch laughed in his fathling's arms and said, "I was not worried at all. Everyone knows pocket fairies are much too fresh for a bridge troll to eat."

Ⴁhe Sᴛoʀy ᴀꜰᴛᴇʀ ᴛhe Sᴛoʀy

The Epilogue

O ur nest is going," Jolly squeaked.
"Our nest is gone," said Gennis.
"We are nestless," whispered Paunch.
Stunned, the Sky Weaver Night Shine pocket fairy family of Middleburg watched as their comfortable, roomy nest crashed to the ground, and a modern, sleek traffic light rose to replace it. Standing close together and peering over the edge of Costard's nest, Marker and Nanda and their three nestlings watched as the pockling crew finished their repairs, dusted off their hands, and carted away what had been their home in the middle of Middleburg. The new, modern, traffic light, small and light, swung easily in the fresh breeze. It was easy to see that this traffic light would never be roomy enough for a growing family of pocket fairies, especially once their wings sprouted.

Undaunted, Marker started to search for a freshly nest for his nestlings as soon as his wing was tight-fixed. First, he checked near the *Gas-N-Go*, but he and Nanda worried that being too close to both Ralph, the spotty-faced pockling, and Feral's flesh scratching gang would prove too much of a temptation for the adventure seeking Paunch, who talked a great deal about their adventures and thought himself ready-fit for new adventures. Marker and Nanda agreed that some measure of quiet would be the best choice for their growing family.

While Marker searched, the Sky Weaver Night Shine family remained with their friend Costard at his gracious invitation. Staying with Costard was both interesting and educational. He taught them more beautiful words, told them of the wonderful sights to be seen once they were rise-high flyers, and then one freshly day he introduced them to a lovely girl mockingbird named Octavia. The pocket fairies knew that it wouldn't be long before Costard would need his sturdy nest in the O of the *Gas-N-Go* sign for nestlings of his own. And they were ready to get settled into a newly nest of their own.

Marker and Nanda, who were very impressed with Gennis' friend, Zoa, invited him to come and live with them in their new home once Marker found it, but Zoa was happy to keep on eye on the pockling Ralph. He thought the newly world of Middleburg an invigorating, interesting place, and because Zoa had no nestlings or wifely of his own yet, he didn't worry too much about Feral's gang. He found the *Gas-N-Go* a curious sort of place to live, with all its pockling comings and goings. He promised Gennis he would visit often and long, and he promised Paunch and Jolly many stories about his adventures in the land of the straight-tall sky grass.

With the help of the Skink Brothers Whooten, who knew a great deal about dragon eggs and real estate in and around Middleburg, Marker finally settled on a truly modern site for their new nest. It was tucked behind a farmer's house. With its window curtains drawn and grass growing around its wheels, it was a spacious home full of nooks, crannies, and close places where a pocket fairy family could feel tight-fast and snugly.

Not only was it roomy, but Marker found the words on the outside of the new nest, printed in a dazzling flourish of blue-black ink, fine and true. The words said *The Sky is the Limit – Travel Trailer and Get Away Home.* Marker thought this name not only inspiring for his young family, but he also thought it appropriate since Gennis, Paunch, and Jolly had proven themselves as brave-daring as any in the Oberlin fairy clan, or any clan for that matter. The brightly sky was indeed the limit for these quick-smart younglings. Nanda agreed, and into the travel trailer they moved—tucking themselves into a storage cubby beneath a breakfast bench.

Gennis, Paunch, and Jolly, in their fairy nest near Middle Street, drank the milk of mice, ate quick-grass bread, practiced their gifting magic, and waited impatiently for their wings to grow.

Glossary of
Pocket Fairy Terms and Characters

Attic sprites: Small wingless cousins of pocket fairies that prefer to live in homes with attics.

Back-before time: Any time before the time we are in right now; yesterday.

Bestly: Extra good; the best.

Bit-small: The opposite of bigly.

Black-white stripleys: Zebras.

Bookly: Having to do with books or pages in a book.

Bridge Trolls: Traditionally, trolls that live under bridges like in the story *Billy Goats Gruff.*

Broom-sweep: A broom.

Brotherling: A boy pocket fairy who has a sisterly or sisterlys.

Carve-sharp: A dangerous feeling or thing.

Chance-luck: Good or bad fortune.

Chantly: A way of speaking when making magic.

Climb-down: A way to climb down, such as a ladder.

Costard: A mockingbird that lives in the letter *O* in the neon sign of the *Gas-N-Go* store.

Croakly: A dry, tight voice.

Cruel-tight: Mean or nasty.

Dankly: A dark, damp place or feeling.

Dare-great: Trying to do something very brave.

Dark-alone: Frightening, lonely darkness.

Day-night: Time passing; the sun rising and setting.

Digging-in-the-dirt-pockling: An electrician from *The Middleburg Power and Light Company*.

Dirtly: Sand, gravel, dirt.

Drizzle Mountain Leprechaun: Leprechauns that live at the foot of Drizzle Mountain in the Scarlet Caves.

Drum-thumping: A pounding, repetitive thumping noise.

Dust-speak: Being able to speak and understand the language of fly specks and dust motes.

Eye-leak: Tears.

Fast-trapped: Being captured or caught.

Fathling: A pocket fairy father.

Feral Flesh-Scratcher: A stray cat, the leader of a group of stray cats that live behind the *Gas-N-Go*.

Firm-steady: Solid and strong.

Flash-white: The brightest white you can imagine.

Flesh-scratchers: Stray cats.

Flutterlys: Butterflies.

Frownly: A grumpy, unsmiling face.

Gas-N-Go: A convenience store located at the corner of Middle Street and Center Avenue in Middleburg.

Gennis Star Milk: Nanda and Marker's oldest nestling.

Gifting magic: A special kind of magic that is unique to each pocket fairy.

Glitter Lakes: A chain of lakes located near the secret Green Glitter Spring.

Godmotherly: A pocket fairy, usually a relative, that has the responsibility to help young pocket fairies learn to fly.

Go-easy: To treat gently.

Grim-dark: A scary, shadowy place, feeling, or situation.

Grumply: Grouchy or out of sorts.

Hard-downly: The ground.

Heart-bound: Connected to other people by love; family love.

Here-now: Right now, right here.

High-mile sailing clouds: Clouds that pocket fairies learn to wind balance on.

Honk-horns: Car horns.

Housely-homes: Pockling houses.

Hug-kissed: Getting a hug and a kiss at the same time.

Hugly: Getting and loving hugs.

Jokely: Being a joker or telling jokes.

Jolly Sky Glint: The youngest sisterly of Paunch and Gennis.

Knack-gifts: Talents and abilities.

Know-not: Ignorant.

Lone-stark: A worried, empty, lonely situation.

Long-tall necklys: Giraffes.

Look-watch: Pay attention.

Luck-joy: A feeling of happiness about some good fortune.

Marker Best Moon: The fathling of the Sky Weaver Night Shine family.

Merfolk: Mermaids and mermen that live in the ocean.

Mischief-magic: Silly dangerous magic.

Monsterly: A loud, frightening creature like a monster; a bulldozer.

Moon-wide: As large as the moon.

Motherly: A mother pocket fairy.

Mousely: Like a mouse.

Muckly: Dirty or messy.

Nanda Star Shimmer: Marker's wifely and the motherly of Gennis, Paunch, and Jolly.

Nestlings: Baby pocket fairies.

Newly time: The modern age.

Oberlin fairy clan: A famous pocket fairy clan known for its brave and daring deeds.

Parentlings: The motherly and fathling pocket fairies.

Pat-kissed: Hugs, kisses, and pats.

Paunch Moon Climb: Nanda and Marker's second nestling and first sonly.

Pocket fairies: One of the smallest of the fairy folk; their name comes from their habit of building their nests in the pockets of humans in the back-before time.

Pocklings: Human beings.

Pointly: Anything that comes to a point like pocket fairy ears.

Poutling: Someone in a bad temper who frets and pouts.

Praise-pat: Letting someone know that they've done a good job with a pat on the back.

Quick-easy: An event that goes much easier than one might expect.

Quick-smart: Being quick about being smart.

Rant-wild: A thrashing terrible rain that comes with a hurricane.

Rider-drivers: People who ride in or drive automobiles.

Rise-higher flyers: Birds.

Rock-strong: Very strong.

Rusher-rumble-bys: Automobiles.

Sad-false: Not true.

Salty: Being saltly.

Set-free: To release someone from a prison or a trap.

Shake-afraid: Being so afraid that you feel shaky.

Sharp-bright: Getting a good idea; being smart.

Sisterly: A female pocket fairy who has a brotherling or brotherlings.

Skink Brothers Whooten: Jut and Frit Whooten Skink who have a relocation company and are friends of Costard.

Skinkly: Being like a skink.

Sky-nest: A pocket fairy nest built in a traffic light.

Sky-straight: Growing tall and straight.

Sleep-dark: Night time.

Sleep-slow: Sleepy or drowsy.

Slickery or slickish: Smooth and scaly like a dragon's skin.

Smushed: Mashed flat.

Snarkly: Rude and grumpy.

Snarl-sharp: Like the pointed teeth of an alley cat; dangerous.

Sneakly: Tricky and sneaky.

Spark-blue: Bright blue with sparkles.

Spinning-horse-mountain-twirly-top: A weather vane on top of a barn roof.

Squinkly: Narrow, squinty eyes.

Stick-bits: Broken branches and sticks.

Stick-tape: Electrical tape.

Stinkling: Someone who is a real stinker.

Stinkly: Being a real stinker.

Stone-still: Being as still as a stone.

Stone-strong trunkleys: Elephants.

Sun-silly: Crazy from too much sun.

Sun-speckles: Freckles.

Swallowers: Snakes.

Terrible spotted skin-grabbers: Owls.

Tight-fast: Safe and secure.

Tight-hold: Staying close or holding on tightly.

Tree stump pixie: Pixies who live in rotted tree stumps and prefer the quiet of the deep woods.

Trouble-bother: Serious problems.

Trovely: Treasure that is hidden.

Twist-twine: String or yarn.

Twitchly: What a flesh-scratcher does with its tail when it is thinking of chasing something.

Up-grown time: Adult.

Uply: High up.

Wait-fast: Stop.

Warm-true: Sincere and real.

Waverly Woods: The birthplace of Nanda and Marker.

Well-wish: Thinking a good thought for others.

Wide-big: The largest place you can imagine.

Wild-salt-zebra-wind: A hurricane.

Wind balancing: When a pocket fairy fathling takes his nestlings out of the nest to balance on mile high sailing clouds so they can be ready to learn to fly.

Word-learning: Studying languages not your own.

Worry-concern: What you feel when you have trouble-bother.

Zoa Help Spirit: A helpful pocket fairy from the continent of Africa.

Acknowledgements

The author would like to thank:

Dr. Ball and Mr. Maginnes, who didn't waste my time or my money; Michelle, Kathy, Joe, Carol and Lisa, who waded through the early drafts and were nice enough to be nice; Ben, Jonathon, and Courtney, my junior editors, for saying things like, "Awesome," and "I liked it;" Paula Kalinoski, my editor and friend, who I strongly suspect believes in pocket fairies in her heart; MyLinda Butterworth and Linda Day for helping me take the "next step" and for teaching me how to make beautiful books; Paula Norris, who I respect for knowing a lot about books and children; Mindy Milton, who has encouraged me from the very beginning; Cherilyn King for holding my feet to the grammar fire; Phillip, my son-in-law, for being honest and feisty; my daughter Heather, who said to Phillip, "Who do you think you are?" when he took a red pen to my manuscript; my hero son Aric, for making me proud; my daughter Maren, for never letting me take myself too seriously and who tried to read my manuscript but kept falling asleep; my son Adam, who always said something I needed to hear and whose insights I respect more than most adults; and my husband Sherwood, who bought me a laptop computer and then wouldn't let me beat it to death with a hammer.

I am heart-bound to each of you.

About the Author

Linda L. Zern

As a young pockling growing up in Middleburg, Linda L. Zern spent many sleep-slow afternoons reading and dreaming. Her love of small and dearly things inspired her to write the story of *The Pocket Fairies of Middleburg*. Mrs. Zern would like to invite her grandchildren and children everywhere to join her in the pleasant reverie that pocket fairies are real, magic is within our grasp, and possibilities are as endless as our wandering dreams.

The author has been spending the last twenty-five years teaching her own four nestlings to read, wonder, and aspire, and trying to decide if pocket fairies are two and one-half inches tall or two and three-eighths inches tall. She was pleasantly surprised to discover that different pocket fairies are of differing heights—just like us.

Mrs. Zern currently lives in Celebration, Florida, with her husbandly named Sherwood (like the forest) and a flesh-scratcher named Charlie. She suspects strongly that her pocket fairy adventures are far from over, and that she has discovered a pixie nest in a stump just past the foot bridge near her home. She plans to wait for the light of a clean, winter moon, hide behind a palmetto bush, and wait for the pixies to swarm.